Gate of Ivory,
Gate of Horn

Gate of Ivory, Gate of Horn

Philip Craig, *1933-*

Published for the Crime Club by
Doubleday & Company, Inc.
Garden City, New York
1969

Excerpts from BEOWULF translated
by Burton Raffel
Copyright © 1963 by Burton Raffel. Reprinted
by permission of The New American Library, Inc.

R 36514

F
C 8447

Library of Congress Catalog Card Number 69–20068
Copyright © 1969 by Philip R. Craig
All Rights Reserved
Printed in the United States of America
First Edition

To My Mother,
Grace Craig,
Who read to us all while the wind blew through the
house.

Gate of Ivory,
Gate of Horn

CHAPTER 1

Across the table Wiglafson peeked again at his hole card and rubbed his right forefinger through his beard. Beside him, his ancient bottle of unspeakably black liquor sat nearly empty and seemed to send some unnamed essence curling into the dark air which, to my dimming eyes, hung like a storm cloud over and about the hulking Scandinavian. Wiglafson's deep-set eyes seemed to gleam bright red beneath his overhanging brows as he flicked his gaze around the table.

To Wiglafson's left, the little man named Relnick lit another cigarette and blew still more smoke into the already heavy air. He was still in the pot, but I wasn't worried about him yet; Wiglafson was my real concern, for I wasn't sure I wanted him to meet the raise. If he was lucky on the fifth card, my fifteen hundred bucks was down the drain; and I was in no shape to lose that kind of dough.

Wiglafson made up his mind and looked down at his pile of bills.

"My money here is not enough, Martingale," he rumbled irritably. His great voice boomed dully in the room.

I looked across at him and said nothing. There was a silence in the room. Wiglafson furrowed his brow, then tipped his bottle to his lips. The rest of us watched him.

"I have my boat," said Wiglafson finally, looking around.

A boat? My tired brain stirred slightly. I flicked my eyes beyond Wiglafson to Farrow, who was standing at the crate that served as the bar. Farrow inclined his head almost imperceptibly. I'd known him long enough to understand what that meant.

"All right," I said. The morning sun was breaking through the curtained window, sending little shafts of swirling light into the room beside Farrow.

"She is moored five blocks down the street if you wish to see her," rumbled Wiglafson, his voice grinding like broken rock.

"All right. What's your proposition?"

"I will give you a share against your wager. A twentieth of her value." His voice was touched with pain.

"Write it down."

Farrow came to the table and gave Wiglafson a pen and a pad of paper. Laboriously, Wiglafson scribbled out a few lines of ancient-looking script, then tore off the sheet and tossed it in the pot.

"I call your bet," he said.

Relnick looked at the cards. Each man at the table had one down and three up. Wiglafson had a king and two jacks showing, and I showed two queens and a ten. Relnick showed a jack and two tens, and was out of luck; Wiglafson had his jacks and I had one of his tens. He turned over his cards and sat back.

"Last card," said Jorgan, who held the deck. He flipped a fifth card first to Wiglafson and then to me.

"Queens bet," said Jorgan, looking at me.

I looked at the spade six I'd gotten; it was no help to me, but then Wiglafson's diamond trey was no good either.

"Three hundred," I said, throwing the last of my money into the pot with a slight flourish.

Wiglafson knew he was locked out, but could not chance

a bluff. If my hole card wasn't another queen, his own high pair would be good.

"I will give you two hundredths of my boat," he said, tight lipped.

"All right," I said.

Farrow came again with the pen and paper, and Wiglafson scribbled another note and tossed it in the pot.

"Call," he said, and I turned over my queen in the hole.

Wiglafson spat out a short word in a tongue I'd never heard.

Behind him, Farrow drew open the curtains and opened the window. Light and salt air streamed in from the Boston Harbor and sent the smoke swirling about the room. Wiglafson jerked around in his chair, his eyes glinting in the dark shadows beneath his brows, "Shut the window, Jacob. This game is not done yet, I think!"

"It may be for you," said Relnick mildly. "You're flat."

Wiglafson swung his red eyes from Farrow to Relnick and leaned toward him, his massive frame dwarfing the smaller man.

"There is money in every town, my little friend! This game of cards will not stop until I, Beorn Wiglafson, have found some of that money and have won back the wagers I have lost here!" His voice rolled out the open window like a foghorn.

Relnick was unintimidated, "Three days is long enough for any poker game," he said. "We could probably all walk to Frisco by the time you came up with any more dough."

Again Wiglafson spat out words I did not know. He turned back to Farrow, who stood with his back to the open window, looking at the table. "What do you say, Jacob? You will give me time to find money, yes?"

Farrow looked at the rest of us and saw that all of us still had our money on the table.

"One hour, Beorn," he said. "The rest of us will eat a bite

and clean up while you go out to rustle up some cash." He pulled out the heavy pocket watch I'd seen him win in Miami a month before and looked at it. "We'll pick up the game at seven."

Wiglafson stared around the room, but no one seemed to be paying any attention to him. Even in the light of the morning sun there seemed to be a darkness around him. Snorting and getting to his feet, he swept his long billed cap from the rack by the door and started toward the hall. At the door he paused and turned to Farrow.

"I will be back," he said.

"All right," said Farrow. Wiglafson thrust out his bearded chin and stomped out of sight.

I stacked my bills and put the two pieces of paper representing seven percent of Wiglafson's boat beside them. My fingers touched the money and I looked at the light streaming in through the window. My mind was turning with the swirlings of smoke in the air, and for the first time since receiving that shocking letter from Aunt Delia, the glimmering of an idea was beginning to take shape in my brain. I felt a tingle of calculated joy tremble through me, but three days of poker had deadened my brain too much for me to know what, exactly, was taking shape in my head. All I could really see clearly was Aunt Delia's letter; everything else was shimmering in the sunlight that lanced in through the window of the room.

At the rim of my mind, someone said, "Come on, kid. Let's get some chow." My mind was in no hurry, but I blinked at the sunlight and looked around. The players, save for Jorgan, who had a thermos and a brown bag of sandwiches before him on the bar, were going out of the door.

"Lock this door when we get out," Farrow was saying to Jorgan. He looked at me, "You coming, kid?"

"Where?"

"Down the street for breakfast. The walk will loosen you up and the grub is good."

"All right." I got up, leaving the money on the table, and followed Farrow out the door. We went down the hall and down the worn stairs at the end of it. At the bottom of the stairs we came out onto Atlantic Avenue. The air was cool, and we hunched our shoulders against the April wind as we started down the street. Ahead of us, Relnick and the others were walking together. Farrow and I walked in silence, feeling our muscles loosen in the morning air and our brains begin to shake off the dullness of sleeplessness and smoke. Images were sharpening inside my skull.

"You're playing over your head, kid," said Farrow suddenly, breaking the silence which normally surrounded him. I wasn't surprised, for I knew he was right. We'd shared too many games down South for him to overestimate me.

"I know," I said, but I wasn't thinking of the game. I was thinking of Aunt Delia's letter.

"You ain't bad," said Farrow, "but you ain't as good as you seem to be in this game either."

"I've had the cards," I said absently.

"That's right, kid." Farrow glanced at me briefly.

I'd found Aunt Delia's letter waiting for me in Miami when I flew in from the Bahamas, where the schooner was registered to avoid complications with the U.S. regulations concerning cruise ships. I was supposed to pick up a new batch of passengers for the schooner, take them out to the Islands, and get them started on their romantic cruise "on a genuine stay-sail schooner through the exotic islands and tropical waters of the historic Caribbean."

At the airport I'd said goodby to Farrow, who'd just completed his annual cruise and was returning to Boston with a small fortune taken from fellow cruisers from St. Paul and Wheeling in friendly on-deck poker games.

"If you get up to Boston, look me up, kid," he said. "We've

usually got a little action going for us up there, and you might enjoy the trip."

"Thanks."

"The boys up there play a little better than they do down here," he said, with the flicker of a smile on his thin face, "but you could probably still make expenses."

We'd taken some of the same suckers in the same games, but I'd gotten dimes to his dollars.

"Maybe I'll see you up there," I said as he walked out to catch his Boston flight. I smiled, but I had no more intention of going to Boston again than I did of taking up knitting. To me, Boston meant Dottie, and Dottie meant Weststock, and Weststock meant disaster. I hadn't enjoyed being given my walking papers by that venerable institution, and wanted nothing more to do with any part of New England. As the first Martingale in a hundred years to flunk out of the college my Calvinistic forefathers had helped to found, I preferred the modest comfort of Caribbean cruise ships, where as deck hand and comforter of ladies old and young I had some choice of pleasures.

But then, at the post office in Miami, I found the letter from Aunt Delia and everything changed. Aunt Delia was in Oil and Steel and, being childless, had always seemed to favor my smiling face to those of her other relatives. I had great confidence in her beneficence, and didn't mind waiting for my share of her inheritance. In view of my certainty, in fact, my irritation at being tossed out of Weststock was mild indeed. What difference would a B.A. make, after all?

Quite a bit, I discovered.

"My dear Luther," Aunt Delia had written in her firm Victorian hand, "Three years ago, when your mother told me that you were leaving college in order to enter the armed services, I was under the impression that you were doing so voluntarily, out of patriotism and a sense of duty. I now discover that you had little choice in the matter.

"As you know, I put considerable stock in the traditions of our family, and am not eager to encourage breaks in those traditions. There has always been a Martingale at West-stock, and, I hope, there always shall be. If I had a son, he would be a Weststock man.

"In hopes of encouraging you, Luther, to reconsider your position as a Weststock dropout, and to take steps to amend your differences with the college, I am taking this opportunity to inform you that your cousin Grafton Martingale will be entering the freshman class at Weststock in the fall, and that, as the first of his generation of Martingales to graduate from the college, he will receive a portion of my estate which I once thought would be yours.

"As you know, I have never liked either young Grafton or his father and I have always liked you. Still, duty is duty, and I can respect only those who perform theirs. I look forward to receiving news of your re-entrance into Weststock.

Love,
Aunt Delia"

Who'd have thunk it!

Ahead of us, Relnick and the others turned into a small neon-lit café. When Farrow and I got inside, Relnick had coffee waiting for us.

"Hello, Jake," said the aproned proprietor who stood beside the table scribbling orders. He nodded to me.

"Hello, George," said Farrow.

From the kitchen at the rear of the café, the smells of food drifted out. I inhaled them and was suddenly very hungry. When George looked at me, I ordered juice, bacon, eggs over light, and toast. I sipped at my coffee while the others talked, but did not listen to them. Their voices, flitting on the periphery of my consciousness, discussed the Rex Sox, Wonderland, and the motor scooters that the Boston Police Department was experimenting with in its patrols of the Common. When their food came, the talking stopped and the men ate in silence, each thinking his own thoughts. Mine were of Dr. Cyril Ashman, chairman of the English department and faculty representative on the admissions committee of Weststock College, Weststock, Mass. The image of him in my mind turned the food tasteless in my mouth.

"And so, ladies and gentlemen," he was saying, pointing with his immaculate hand at the blackboard he'd just spent an hour filling with scrawls and squiggles, "we see that by first adopting a set of symbols such as these to represent the main accents of the verse, we may go beyond the essentials which have occupied us thus far and enter into a full description of hypermetric alliteration."

He paused, and beside me, Dottie, his niece, rapidly recorded his every word in her notes. Catching his cold eye upon me, I doodled intently in my note book. In the hall, a bell buzzed dully. The professor reluctantly closed his briefcase.

"Tomorrow, then, we will discuss the supplementary alliteration that occurs in crossed or transverse patterns."

The class, poised for escape, waited for the sigh he emitted at the end of each lecture, heard it, and fled from the room. Beside me, Dot, slim, myopic, and now six weeks pregnant, jostled out of the classroom with me.

"Have you told him yet?" I asked.

She looked at me coldly, "No, not yet, Luther."

I was troubled by an outdated sense of honor, but not troubled enough to suggest marriage, "I hope you know what you're doing," I said.

"Don't worry. I've found a perfectly good place to go in New York. Uncle Cyril has a conference down there next week, and I'm going down with him. While he's taking care of his business, I'll tend to mine." Her voice was precise and expressionless. She was a lovely girl, but aside from that one liquor-warmed hour six weeks before, when she'd still seen me as the last of a grand old line of Weststock scholars and had somehow fallen from the icy grace of her own inherent intellectualism, I'd never known her to be warm. She was too much like her uncle; perhaps because he, as her only kin, guarded her so closely that she took his very form.

"You're sure you'll be okay," I said, feeling a flood of relief. "After all, it was my fault too. . . ."

"All I'll need from you is two hundred dollars," she said.

"That's cheap," I said, surprised.

"It's half the fee," she snapped. "I have no intention of forcing you to pay for everything when you are only half responsible."

Farewell, paternal pension. I'd have to play a bit more poker in the graduate lounge to make expenses, but all in all, I was getting out cheap.

"You're sure, now . . ." I said, my voice trailing off.

"I'm sure, Luther."

But she didn't come back from New York after the conference, and the following Monday I received an icy request from Dr. Cyril Ashman to see him in his office immediately. I had a sense of doom as I passed through the door into his office and took the chair he gestured toward. He wasted no time. Leaning across his desk, his long fingers locked in a two handed fist in front of his chin, he gave me a sad choice:

"Mr. Martingale, I care nothing at all for the history of your name at this institution, so please make no threats. My niece is, at this moment, in a private hospital in New York, recovering from an abortion. You are the father of the aborted fetus. The hospital where the operation took place contacted me when complications arose, and Dottie, under sedation, admitted that you were the father. Close your mouth, Mr. Martingale."

I closed my mouth.

"I have no intention of wasting words with you, so listen carefully. You are in two of my classes this semester. At the end of the semester, you shall have failed those two courses if you choose to stay at the college that long. With two failures on your record, you will be dismissed from the college and will have to wait a year before applying for re-admittance. I am on the admissions committee. As long as I am on that committee, you will never re-enter Weststock.

"Your other choice, Mr. Martingale, is to withdraw now, this very day, from college. If you choose that course, you will avoid the stigma of two failures on your academic record. Frankly I would prefer it if you left immediately. I have no wish to see you in my classes for the rest of this term, and I would prefer it if Dottie did not have to see you when she returns."

There was a cold knot in my chest, and my eyes were tight and aching.

"I'll stay," I said. And I did. Dot only missed a week of school, and looked quite well when she got back. I handed in every paper on time in both of her uncle's courses, and received quite cold and objective criticism on all of them. Once or twice he even complimented me on my analysis. In the spring I packed my things and joined the Army. A month later I received my grades from Weststock and a letter regretting that the college was obliged to drop me, for the time, from its academic rolls. Dottie and I wrote regularly.

Farrow, Relnick, and the others sat at the table over their after-breakfast coffee and lit new smokes. Outside, the street was beginning to come to life. A police cruiser drifted past and trucks were beginning to rumble by. The players drank the last of their coffee and pushed back from the table. George came out from the kitchen and moved behind the cash register at the door. One by one, the players paid their bills and went out onto the sidewalk. In a loosely knit group we walked back to the game.

Jorgan let us in, and we moved back to the table. It was five minutes till seven.

"Wiglafson been back?" asked Farrow.

Jorgan shook his head. At the table Relnick picked up a deck and began to deal himself a hand of solitaire. I let my left hand touch the bills in front of me. I had never had so much money in my life, but my fingers seemed more interested in the bits of scribbled paper Wiglafson had given me. A tingle ran up my arms and stirred my brain when I touched the sheets of paper. A cloud gathered in my mind, hardened, and almost became an idea. Somewhere beyond the windows of the room a clock began ringing out the hour. A picture of Dr. Cyril Ashman's thin hard face formed in my mind for an instant, but then I was listening to the heavy sound of footsteps in the hall, and I looked up to see Wiglafson come through the door. His eyes were hot.

"Well?" asked Farrow.

"I found no one. At least no one with money."

"Tut, tut," clicked Relnick. Wiglafson looked at him and Relnick was quiet.

"I have this," said Wiglafson, and he produced a leather purse. Opening the top of the bag, he spilled a pile of irregular coins on the table. The coins thudded down, dark against the table top. Farrow picked one up, looked at it, put it to his mouth and bit. He smiled and shook his head.

"Not me," he said, "I have no use for gold coin."

"It is good coin," rumbled Wiglafson.

"I know," said Farrow. No one else said anything. Wiglafson looked at every man individually, his face ancient and angry as his eyes moved around the room.

"By the gods!" he said. He brought out his wallet and

dug out a document from one of its inner pockets. Holding it in one massive hand, he waved it over the table.

"This is my boat. She is worth twenty thousand." He looked into my eyes, "I still own ninety-three percent of her, ya? That should be worth money to you."

Relnick looked tempted, but then shook his head. "I ain't no sailor. I don't need no sailboat."

Jorgan shook his head, "No. If she was a fisherman, I might be interested, but I don't need no sailboat."

Wiglafson turned to Farrow, "What about you, Jacob? You know what she is worth."

Farrow stood with his hands on the sill of the open window. "What would I do with a sailboat?"

Wiglafson's face reddened. His massive hand began to crumple the paper in his fingers. Beside him, Jorgan pushed his chair slightly back from the table. Wiglafson turned and stared down at him.

I said, "I'll give you two thousand dollars for another twenty percent."

Wiglafson stared at me across the table.

"Just write it down," I said, hearing a ringing in my ears as I spoke. I rested my hand on the bills in front of me. Across the room Farrow was looking at me blankly.

"Ten percent," said Wiglafson.

I took my hand off the money.

Wiglafson's mouth wrinkled snakelike behind his beard, and he slapped the paper against his other hand, "Very well, by the gods, twenty percent."

"Sit down," said Relnick, sweeping up the cards before him and shuffling them.

Wiglafson sat down in his old chair. Farrow brought the pad of paper and the pen, and Wiglafson scribbled again and gave me the paper. I counted out twenty hundred dollar bills and handed them across. I now had nearly nine hundred dollars left. Almost enough to pay the taxes on Aunt Delia's gatehouse.

"My deal," said Farrow, sitting down between Wiglafson and Jorgan. The sixth and seventh players, nondescript men both of whom were named Smith and both of whom had played nondescript poker for the past three days, off and on, pulled their chairs nearer the table and the game got under way.

At one o'clock the next morning, I owned seventy-seven percent of Wiglafson's boat and had nearly two thousand dollars in front of me. Better yet, my brain was getting its second wind and an idea was taking shape in the dark cloud that hung between my ears.

CHAPTER 2

The two Smiths had finally quit bucking the game and had withdrawn to the bar to watch. My eyes were red and throbbing as I watched two hundred of my dollars being added to the growing pile at Farrow's elbow. Across the table Wiglafson poured the final dregs from his foul black liquor bottle down his throat and scowled across at me as though from the depths of time.

"I'm out," said Jorgan tiredly.

I dug through my bills and found a ten. I gave it to Jorgan and watched the others at the table do the same. Jorgan nodded and got up. "I'll go down and rustle up some sandwiches and coffee," he said.

"Good," said Farrow. It was the first word he had spoken in over an hour.

"Deal," growled Wiglafson, lighting his acrid pipe. In the swirl of smoke, his face was dark and old.

At three o'clock I won a small pot with a pair of aces and began a streak of good hands. Farrow and Relnick began to drop early to ride out the storm, but Wiglafson, tired and angry and a heavy loser, played hard with second-best hands. At six in the morning I gave him a thousand dollars and watched as Wiglafson wrote out a bill of sale for the ketch and had it witnessed by Relnick and Farrow. I took the bill of sale and the ownership papers from Wiglafson and sat back in my chair. Wiglafson's face was immobile as stone.

"Time for breakfast," said Farrow.

"No," growled Wiglafson, his voice rumbling out of his beard. "We go on, I say." He slapped out a round of cards face down.

Farrow looked at Relnick and me.

"Okay by me," said Relnick. I nodded. My mind was singing.

❦ Wiglafson dealt the second cards face up. Farrow's queen was high. He tipped up the corner of his hole card and pushed five dollars into the center of the table. I had a jack showing, but I paired my king in the hole on the third card and took a hundred dollars from Wiglafson. At eleven o'clock, on luck alone, I filled a small straight and cleaned Wiglafson down to his last ten dollars. I pointed to the bag of gold coins.

"I'll play you for that now," I said.

Wiglafson's eyes were ageless. He looked at his three aces, tore them in two, kicked back his chair and stalked from the room. The two Smiths and Jorgan, who had been alternating between dozing, bringing food and coffee, and watching the game, looked after him. The only sound in the building was that of Wiglafson's heavy footsteps going down the hall and then down the stairs. The door leading to the street slammed distantly; then the building was quiet. Relnick fingered the torn cards and then pushed back his chair.

"Well, I guess that's it," he murmured.

"You're lucky, kid," said Farrow, getting up and stretching.

I looked at my money and at the papers that made me the owner of a boat I'd never seen. I had a lot of money; over two thousand dollars. I smiled up at Farrow.

"I'll play with you until midnight if you want," I said, "but then I'm going to stop."

Relnick got up and began to pick up his money, "Mister Martingale, I wouldn't play with you any more in this game unless you paid me. I'll wait awhile and let your luck run off."

Farrow nodded agreement, "We've had enough, kid. You take your money and get some sleep."

"All right," I said. I picked up my money and papers and put it in various pockets. I got my jacket from the rack by the door and threw it over my shoulder.

"So long," I said.

"So long, kid," said Farrow.

• Halfway down the hall I turned around and went back. The men in the room were at the bar pouring whiskey into paper cups. They looked up as I came through the door.

"Do any of you know where my boat is?"

"Sure," said Jorgan. "When you get to the street, turn left and go down five blocks and turn left again. Keep walking and you'll come to a dock. She's tied up out at the end."

"Thanks." I turned and went down to the street. The sun was hot and the traffic was heavy. I turned left and began walking. A police cruiser slowed as it approached me and the cops inside looked me over casually. I knew I was a little seedy in my wrinkled clothes and three-day beard, but the money in my pockets made me lighter than air. I walked slowly on and saw the cruiser pick up speed and go on up the street.

I stepped onto the dock and paused as a weathered man came out of the door of a shack carrying a box of tinned goods. The man crossed in front of me and stepped aboard a trawler tied alongside the dock. I waited while the man went below and stowed his load. When he came back on deck, I was waiting for him at the gangplank.

"I'm looking for a boat." I dug into a pocket and produced

a wad of money, put it back and dug into another pocket this time producing the boat's papers. "Her name's the *Gate of Horn,*" I said, looking at the papers.

"What?" asked the fisherman, reluctantly taking his eyes from the money filled pocket.

"The *Gate of Horn.*"

"Oh, Wiglafson's boat. She's way out there at the end of the wharf. But he ain't around yet this morning."

"That's all right," I said, "I've already seen him. Thanks." I walked on out along the dock. Beyond, in the harbor, an aircraft carrier was moving slowly out to sea. Squinting through the haze, I made out her name: *Wasp.* And I remembered that south, on Cape Kennedy, two astronauts were preparing for another rocket flight into space. The dock reached out into the harbor. Fishing boats in from the Banks were moored bow to stern in worn succession beside it. I walked past them with the smell of salt and fish in my nostrils and the sounds of the harbor in my ears.

At the end of the pier I stopped and looked down at the boat tied there. She lay still in the calm oily water, her woodwork dark and warm in the nooning sun. Across her stern in a swirl of gold leaf was her name: *Gate of Horn.* I stood on the dock and studied her, feeling my heart thump. She was everything I might have wished: a boat made for ocean cruising.

She was thirty-six or thirty-seven feet long from stem to stern and was broad in the beam and heavy. Double-ended, with a tiller rather than a wheel, her lines were those of a North Sea pilot boat. She was ketch-rigged, gaffed, and her standing and running lines were stout. Everything about her suggested strength rather than speed, endurance rather than grace. She was, I saw, no spring chicken either, but how my heart thumped when I looked at her.

I swung down a short ladder from the dock and stepped aboard her. Her solidity impressed me; she was no slight thing, to be tossed about in an evening breeze or to bob beneath a maiden's foot. Her deck was neat and shipshape; Wiglafson might be no poker player, but he kept a trim ship.

Both the fore and main hatches were locked, so I peeked in through the portholes of the cabin to see what I could see. Below, everything was as neat as above deck, and Wiglafson went up still another step in my estimation. Be careful of your biases, I thought, not all good sailors are good men. Or good poker players. Or vice versa.

I got off my knees and worked my way around the boat, tugging on her standing rigging and running lines. Which line did what? I found her main and mizzen halyards and two more for her foresails. The sheets for all four sails led back to winches on either side of the cockpit. The cockpit itself was rather small, which satisfied me well enough; less space for a cockpit meant more room below. And the decks were wide enough for passengers to lounge about, if any lounging passengers were aboard.

Not bad, I thought, and looked up at the masts. They were short and heavy and well stayed and shrouded. At the top of the mainmast a small pennant fluttered in the wind.

"Well, what ya think of her?" asked a voice from the dock behind me. A casual, friendly voice, I thought, and so I turned slowly and looked up at the man who had spoken.

"Well, she won't win any races, but she'll still be afloat when a lot of others are under water."

The man on the dock nodded and puffed on his briar. He was past middle age and wore a pea coat and cap.

"You a friend of Beorn?"

Beorn? Wiglafson. "I know him," I said.

"He ain't generally around this time of day."

"When do you expect him?"

"Hell, I don't expect him," said the man, "I work down there." He gestured toward the land and blinked down at

me as the smoke from his pipe swirled into his eyes. "Beorn
pays me a couple of bucks to keep an eye on things when
he's away."

"Ah," I said, "you're a watchman then."

The man nodded agreeably. "That's about it," he said.

I climbed up the ladder and flashed my teeth in a wide
smile. "My name's Martingale and you're just the man I
want to see. Take a look at these." I dug out the boat's papers
and the bill of sale.

The watchman obligingly read the papers and then
handed them back in mild surprise. "You got yourself a good
boat there, Mr. Martingale. She's old but she's stout enough
to outlast you." He shook his head, "Beorn must have been
some hard up for money. The old *Gate* sure meant a hell of
a lot to him."

"He was hard up, all right," I said, sadly. "Look here, Cap,
how long have you been around these parts?"

"Why, all my life," he said, rather proudly.

"Well, I'll tell you what," I lied, "I'm a stranger here myself and I want to move this boat up to Gloucester. How do
I get there?"

"Why, nothin' to it. You just follow the main channel out
and head off up the . . . say now, why don't you bring out
your charts so I can show ya?"

"Can't, worse luck," I growled.

"Why not? Beorn's got charts of half the god damned
world down there in his chart locker."

I half turned away and scuffed embarrassedly at the dock
with my foot. "Well, dammit, when I went on board I was in
such a blasted rush that I stepped on that cleat there,
slipped, and damned near went overboard. I had the keys
to the boat in my hand and dropped them in the drink when
I was grabbing for a handhold." I gestured irritably at my
shoes, "No damned business going on board in leather shoes
in the first place. Serves me right."

"Hell," said the man, with a sympathetic chuckle, "no problem there. You wait here a second. We'll have those hatches off some sudden."

I watched him trot down the dock toward shore. Hurry up, I thought, poker debts aren't legal in Massachusetts, and when Wiglafson finds his lawyer, he'll be down here in a flash.

The man was back in less than two minutes. He carried a hacksaw which he waved triumphantly.

"That'll do it," I said, and I went on board the *Gate of Horn* and sawed off the padlocks on her hatches. Sliding the main hatch forward, I stepped down into the main cabin and turned hurriedly to the engine. The engine was my only hope; I couldn't plan on taking her out under sail; she was too big for me to handle green in a busy harbor. The big Gray Marine lay tucked comfortably aft under the cockpit. Like the rest of the boat, it was old but well maintained. I found the starter, worked on the wires, then stood up and stuck my head out of the hatch.

"This thing fueled up?"

The man on the dock nodded, "Yep. Beorn kept her ready to go. She takes about thirty gallons and she's filled up."

"Water, too?"

"Tanks ain't full 'cause Beorn likes it fresh when he leaves. Enough to see you to Gloucester, though."

"Good." I glanced about and crossed the cabin to a locker. Inside, right where they should be, were Wiglafson's charts. I looked through them and found the three I wanted: one of Boston Harbor, one of the North Shore, and one of Gloucester Harbor. Closing the locker I went out into the cockpit and on up onto the dock. There I spread the charts and the watchman of Wiglafson's boat showed me my present position.

"From here, ya go out and then bear to starboard at about a hundred degrees. You hold that until you get down

here off of Pier Two or Three. There you bring her a bit
more to the southard—about a hundred and thirty degrees,
maybe—until you see this flashin' red buoy here. Once you're
there, you're in the main channel and on your way. Bear
to eastward out on the President Roads till you pass the
point of Deer Island. From there, ya bear to the northard
toward Finns Ledge and on out onto the Sound. . . ."
The man's fingers flew over the charts. He had me coming
into Gloucester Harbor in less than a minute. I watched with
half of my mind while the other half listened for footsteps on
the dock behind us. Wiglafson was taking his time, thank
God. Maybe he thought the padlocks would be enough, or
that I was still in the game up the street.

". . . Then you round in through here," said the man,
"and there you are. Safe in Gloucester." He leaned back on
his heels and looked up at me. I picked up the charts and
rolled them.

"Gee, thanks a lot," I said, shaking his hand. "You've
been a great help."

I went on board the boat and lay the charts in the cockpit. Time was running out. I grinned up at the man, as if
eager to get out onto blue water, "Well, let's see if she
goes," I said and went below to cross the ignition wires.

The motor caught and I breathed a grateful sigh. The
boat scarcely quivered from the vibrations of the engine. At
low throttle I put her gently into gear and felt her push
against her mooring lines. I shifted into reverse and let her
push back again. The pilings to which she was secured
squeaked slightly as she strained against them. Satisfied, I
threw her out of gear.

Aft, I loosed her stern line and flipped it off the piling.
At the bow, my helper, who apparently had cast off Wiglafson more than once, tossed the bowline onto the deck and
held the forestay.

"Cast her off," I called, taking the tiller and pushing the gearshift forward.

The man pushed on the forestay and the bow of the boat swung slowly away from the dock. I notched the throttle up a bit and the boat curled gently away from the dock. Ahead of her, a dragger came poking out from the moored boats on my right, but there was enough clearance for both of us and I fell in behind the fisherman and headed out into the harbor.

A hundred yards from the dock, I turned and looked back. My pea-jacketed friend was not watching me, but had turned and was looking back toward shore. Pounding out along the dock Wiglafson was running and waving his arms. Behind him, a smaller man clutching a briefcase was scurrying along in his wake. Wiglafson arrived beside the watchman and loomed over him, gesturing toward the boat as she slid away from him out into the harbor.

Engrossed in the scene on the dock, I narrowly missed a tug, received an angry hoot from her whistle, and thereafter was only able to cast occasional glances astern. For a while there was much waving of arms between Wiglafson and the watchman, and then long looks after the retreating boat were accompanied by animated conversation. My last look, before I swung south and passed out of sight, was of Wiglafson and his presumed lawyer hurrying shoreward with the watchman walking behind scuffing at the dock with his shoes.

He's told them what he knows, I thought, and they'll either try to get a boat to catch me here, or they'll meet me at Gloucester. So far, so good. I whistled as I moved south into the stream of boats to sea. At the President Roads, where the chart showed I must turn east to clear for Gloucester, I turned southwest instead and pushed the throttle higher as I passed Castle Island and bore into Dorchester Bay. An hour later I tucked the *Gate of Horn* into a finger pier amid a forest of masts. The manager of the yard wanted more than he deserved, but even that was an insignificant portion of my poker winnings so I paid it with a smile. I also bought two padlocks and secured the hatches. Then I phoned for a cab and took it back to Boston.

When I got to my hotel, I showered and fell into bed. Things were falling into place rather well. Better than I had expected, really. The boat, especially, was an unanticipated bonus. I wound my travel-alarm beside the bed and made sure that the alarm button was pushed in. I did not want to wake up in the morning. I pulled a pillow over my head and let my mind slide down into darkness. I'd been without sleep for nearly four days and was deathly tired. My last vision was of the boat, floating golden in the gathering darkness of sleep.

. . . Cyril Ashman's private obsession was fairly well known, actually, to most of his students. In spite of his efforts to keep it to himself, it kept creeping into his lectures or dropping casually into conversation: He believed that Beowulf, the hero of the long poem everyone is forced to read in high school, was a real person.

"It's idiotic, of course," I overheard a young member of the English department say to another, "but there's no way to prove it one way or another."

"You mean he may actually be right?" asked his companion.

"He may be, but damned few other people in the field think so. The funniest part, really, is the way he tries to keep the notion to himself. He's too good a scholar to publicly advertise his notion; he knows he can't really prove it because he hasn't the hard evidence. But he has written about it a good deal in the journals."

"Ah."

"Got his fingers burned a bit, too. Several refutations

from high places and some sarcasm from the young turks. He refuses to give in, though. Keeps hounding the societies for funds for a trip abroad, I understand."

"Any luck?"

"Not that I know of."

"Ah, well. Not my field, really. I'm seventeenth century, myself. Good money for that period. I have a grant that will take me over to London for the summer. . . ."

"Splendid. . . ."

Their voices trailed away as they passed down the hall toward their offices. At that time, early in my sophomore year at Weststock, I'd not crossed swords with Ashman, and felt a little sorry for him. I looked after the retreating instructors and hoped that the Ashman would show them up after all; that he would find the money for his trip abroad and prove to a doubting world that he was right and they were wrong.

A month later, Dottie, his dark-haired niece, succumbed to my Cutty Sark and her own imagination. Six weeks after that, I began to change my mind about her uncle, and by the time summer came I hated him with a passion only equaled by his hatred of me. In the Army, I wrote regularly to Dot out of guilt and curiosity at first, but later out of interest and animosity for her uncle. I read, then, of her passage through her undergraduate studies and into graduate school, and wrote of my own passage through the Army and into a life as crewman aboard passenger schooners running out of the Bahamas.

When she started for her Ph.D., I had found my cranny in the Caribbean, romancing secretaries from Albany and playing profitable card games with balding men from Ames or St. Paul. I'd met Farrow for the first time when Dot wrote about the manuscripts the department had gotten hold of, and I'd learned not to buck him hand to hand when she wrote of the chart. I read the journals when I was in port, and noted with satisfaction that Ashman's new discovery was dismissed as a forgery by everyone who bothered to write about it. One wag attached the title "Ashman's Folly" to the whole affair, and published a poem entitled "The Courtship of a Geatish King" to be sung to the tune of "The Big Rock Candy Mountain." I memorized the song and sang it to bewildered maidens on the schooner's decks beneath tropic skies.

Still, it was, for me, a private rapture only. Knowledge of the doctor's despair served me no useful purpose until after I received Aunt Delia's letter. From then on, it became important for good, solid, pragmatic, American reasons: dollars. In my Miami hotel room, while I ground my teeth and envisioned Aunt Delia's dollar bills, rightfully mine, flying, winged, into the outstretched hands of Cousin Grafton, whom I did not know but hated nevertheless, it suddenly occured to me that Cyril Ashman's private obsession and professional humiliation might, if I were careful, be turned to my advantage.

Cooler, I began to plan. . . .

CHAPTER 3

Dottie opened the door, said hello, and let me in. She wore a sweatshirt and dungarees. Very functional. Her hair was tied back in a knot.

"Hello, Dot," I said, puffing.

"Sit down, Luther."

"Thanks." I did.

"Four days late, and you try to make it up in the last hundred yards. Characteristic."

I smiled at her. She was a cold fish, but she was lovely when she was angry. Slim and prim, she twirled her glasses in one hand and looked darkly down at me.

"I have news . . ." I began.

"I have news for you too," she snapped. "I have three papers to write, and I plan to get them written. I wasted an evening waiting for you to make your appearance and I have no intention of wasting another. What happened to you, anyway? Where have you been?"

"I got in a poker game."

She put her hand to her forehead and leaned back against her paper- and book-strewn desk. "A poker game," she said to the bust of Shakespeare that sat vacant-eyed on her bookcase. Then she set her glasses on the end of her nose and stared hotly over them at me, "You make me sick. If you must play poker, it's all right with me; but for heaven's sake call me next time so I can make other plans. I have other things to do than wait around for you to show up!"

What a fine body she had! Too bad she'd turned it off. After she'd come back from the hospital in New York, I'd made a couple of tentative tactile advances to her, just to show that I was still the same fine guy I was before, but she would have none of it, and I'd soon stopped trying. In the years since then, there had, as far as I knew, been no variation in the physical rigidity she maintained. Only sight and sound seemed important to her sensually, and those only because they brought her food for her mind. Even now, she was angry only because I'd caused her to lose half a day's study.

"Come over here, Dottie, love," I said, holding out my arms, "and I'll comfort you with kisses."

"You did that once before, remember?" She did not move from the desk. She was going to make some library a fine wife.

"Let me explain the poker game, then," I said.

"Go on."

"I intended to see you four days ago, just like I said in my letter. But then, while I was hitching up from Miami I got hooked in this little game in Baltimore, see?, and I lost about nine tenths of the money I started North with.

"Now I have an idea I want to discuss with you, but I had to have some money first. So when I got into Boston I looked up an old friend and got into a little game to see if I could get back a little of the money I lost in Baltimore. . . ."

What a fictitious-sounding story. And it was true, too.

"Well," she said, "did you succeed in regaining the family fortune?"

"That I did. In fact, I got luckier than I ever did before. I won just what I need to get back into Weststock."

She looked honestly pained, "Luther, I'm sure there are a lot of other schools. . . ."

"I want back into Weststock. I'm not interested in going anywhere else."

She sighed, "Oh, Lute, why are you so stubborn? You know you'll never get back in there."

"It's a matter of pride," I said with the hint of temper in my voice. "But you're right. I'm not likely to get back into Weststock as long as the esteemed chairman of the English department has his back up. And he's still on the admissions committee, too, the old bastard."

"Now don't be mad at Uncle Cyril," she said. "It wasn't his fault that you seduced me, you know. . . ."

"I know," I said, remembering.

". . . And what was he supposed to do, anyway? Just let it pass? What would you do, Luther, if some young man stole your only niece's virtue?"

"It wasn't exactly theft," I said.

"Well, theft or not, I dare say you would have done just about what Uncle Cyril did: You'd get rid of the young man and hush the whole thing up."

I was tired of the whole story. For five years I'd had time to brood about the incident and its consequences, and I had never lost my distaste for Cyril Ashman. "The problem with your four-eyed uncle," I said, "is that he mixes his professional life with his personal one. He flunked me cold in two courses just to get rid of me, the old bastard."

"What would you have preferred? To have him shoot you or something? He's of the old school, you know. If you'd wanted to, you could have gone on to school somewhere else. He just wanted you out of Weststock, that's all."

"Fat chance of that," I said, knowing perfectly well that she was right. "Who'd want a Weststock dropout?"

"Anybody."

"You?" I quirked an eyebrow.

"Any college," she amended, coolly.

I smiled, "That's my Dot. But now let's drop all that, shall we? Because I have something that just may get me back into Weststock after all."

She looked at me with suspicious interest. I watched her for a while, waiting for her to ask, and finally she did. "Well, don't just sit there. Tell me what you're talking about."

"A boat," I said, savoring the word. "A little double-ender quite capable of crossing the Atlantic and sailing along the Swedish coast with, say, a half dozen people and a fair supply of digging equipment."

I sat back and watched her face.

Her myopic eyes widened as the implications of the news sifted through to her. "Uncle Cyril's project . . ." she said.

It was a pleasure to see some sign of emotion on her fine fair face.

"That's right," I said. "Dear Uncle Cyril's long postponed and highly fanciful project to find the tomb of Beowulf and prove to a doubting world that he's always been right and they've always been wrong. He was planning it before I ever got to Weststock, and from what you've been writing in your letters and what I've been reading in those blasted dull journals, I know he's still planning it. But you know and I know that he's got about as much chance as a snowball in hell of ever getting the thing done. He's sounded out every organization he can for money and has gotten nothing. He needs a boat, a man to sail it, and a crew to help him with the digging, if he ever finds anywhere to dig, which in my mind is not too likely. All that takes money, Dottie my dear, and unless he gets some, he's all through."

I was relishing the idea. I'd known before I left Florida that the key to getting back into Weststock lay in Ashman himself, and that the key to any man is his weakness. In poker you find a man's weakness, make him think it's his strength, if you make him conscious of it at all, and then use it for your own purposes to milk him dry. Ashman had two weaknesses: Beowulf, and his niece, Dottie, the apple of his professorial eye. Dottie, in turn, had one weakness of her own that I could use: affection for her uncle. I hoped to use both when I started north, but the winning of the boat had crystalized my thinking into a particular plan. I'd been going over it all afternoon, and now I was saying it aloud, listening to the sound of it for the first time, and watching Dot, who listened to me.

"Uncle Cyril is in a tough position," I went on. "He's been at Weststock since the year Ape, and has tenure up to his neck, probably, so he won't be fired. But, on the other hand, a college like Weststock isn't really going to be too happy for too long if the head of its English department is the laughingstock of the academic world, which Uncle Cyril might well become, if he keeps pushing his private lunacy about Beowulf." I looked hard at Dot, "Am I right so far?"

She nodded, looking rather unhappy. "Yes, he is under quite a bit of pressure just now. . . . He's a fine scholar, Lute. . . ."

"He *was* a fine scholar, maybe, but he hasn't done anything original in fifteen years as far as I can tell. He just gets more and more hung up on this Beowulf thing. He's on the ropes," I said, "and he's got to get off of them, or else."

"Don't be so vindictive," she said. "If he ever does get his project financed, and if he's right in thinking the tomb is where he thinks it is, he'll be at the top of his field again."

"Personally," I said, "I don't care if he gets the medal of honor or if he drops dead. Right at the moment, I've got something he needs as bad as he's ever needed anything: I've got a boat and some money, and I can dig as well as the next guy. It's April now, and if I leave the States within a couple of weeks, I can have the boat and gear waiting for him in Sweden or Denmark or wherever he likes when he gets out of school in June."

"And what will you get out of it, Luther?"

Bless her. I leaned toward her, "Just what you think: In exchange for my services, I'll want him to get me back into Weststock in the fall." She opened her mouth, but I hushed her with a raised hand and went on, "He got me out and he can get me in. A recommendation from him, especially since he was the guy who flunked me out in the first place, would open the door, and after that, the ancient and honorable Martingale name should do the rest. It's a simple deal: I get my shot at Weststock, and Uncle Cyril gets his shot at that long-lost tomb of Beowulf that's lodged there in his head."

I paused and there was a silence in the room. Outside, the cars moved along the streets of Back Bay, bleating occasionally at offending pedestrians.

"He'll have a summer to hunt and dig," I said, finally. "That ought to be enough time to prove his theory out one way or another."

"It sounds very neat, Luther," said Dot, finally, "but you've forgotten one thing. Uncle Cyril isn't like you. He's too old fashioned to make a deal with you after what he thinks you did to me. He'll never agree to a plan like yours even if it means that he never gets to look for the tomb. I'm not sure you understand that part of his character: He's honor bound not to deal with you. By sullying me, you sullied him." She looked at me defiantly, but I wasn't about to argue with her, even though I had my private reservations about Uncle Cyril's honor code. Instead, I slid into part two of the argument.

"How important do you think this idea of his really is to him?" I asked. "And how important is it to you?"

Her eyes narrowed, and she reset her glasses firmly on her fine thin nose. "To him it's everything, as you know. He's been at the library poring over that manuscript collection for the past three years, and he's sure he's on to something. . . ."

"And to you?"

"Well, of course it's important to me too. He's been very depressed by his failure to get backing, and I'm worried about him. He looks older than he should. . . ."

"You'd like to see him get a shot at the tomb, then, right?"

Her eyes were dark slits behind her glasses, "All right, Lute; what do you have in mind? I have a sudden feeling that you are trying to be tricky again."

I straightened my crooked smile into a smooth curve. "Three questions. First, would you be willing to go to Sweden this summer as part of the crew your bastardly uncle will need if he takes me up on my offer?"

She thought for a while. Then slowly nodded, "Yes, I could do that. I'd want to be with him, in fact."

"And with me, of course."

She smiled coldly and shrugged a feline shoulder.

"Yes. And with you, too, of course."

What a cool witch she was. For five years she'd remained my friend, but had kept her sexual distance. I could look but not touch. And how tempting a morsel! I wondered if she calculated it all or if it was the work of dark gods.

"Second question," I said. "Do you love me in September as you did in May?"

Her teeth were like ice, "I never loved you, Luther."

"It doesn't really matter," I smiled. "Next question: Will you marry me, Dottie dear?"

Her glasses fell off onto the desk. I watched her Adams apple bob. I'd caught her off guard for the first time in five years.

"Are you serious?" she gasped. And then, "Why, I never . . ."

"Oh yes you did," I corrected, "but that's neither here nor

there. The past is dead and we'll leave it buried. But now, before you respond to my proposal, please use that famous brain of yours and consider the following things. If you say Yes, you have ample opportunity to say No later before the deed is done. This will be especially assured if we set the date for, say, next October or November. In the meantime, dear Uncle Cyril will have been given an honorable out from the moral dilemma he might otherwise be caught in if faced with the prospect of accepting the offer I intend to make him. After all, if the cad who, if I may use your phrase, stole his darling niece's virtue, marries her, he is doing right by her isn't he? . . . I . . . He . . . I would be doing the honorable thing, right? Even somebody as stuffy as Uncle Cyril could ask for no more than that, could he?

"And think of the benefits that could be derived as a consequence of such a promised union of lovers: Uncle Cyril could go off hunting Beowulf's tomb, the wronged damsel could be redeemed and honored in the eyes of kith and kin, and Luther Martingale, repentant sinner, could do the American thing and go back to college for his old B.A., thus giving his saddened mother a joy previously denied her."

I stopped. There was silence in the room while Dot found her glasses and put them on. "This is mad," she muttered. She started walking around and around her desk, pausing every now and then to look at me. I looked as attractive as I could.

"Look," I said, after a while, "I'll ask on bended knee, if you prefer. I'll even marry you in October, if you want, even though I don't want to obligate you to that course of action . . ."

"What did you have in mind instead?" she asked suspiciously.

"Nothing! What you'll really be doing is giving Uncle Cyril a chance to go off to Scandinavia with a clear conscience. Afterward, when he's back home and I'm back in Weststock, you can renounce the engagement or whatever it is that a girl does when she decides not to go through with it." Actually I couldn't see anything wrong with marrying her if that was what she wanted. She was a sexy wench by any standards, and was bright too. She could always get a good day's pay teaching somewhere. "We can really get married, if that's what you want. The only disadvantage I see to marrying you is your prospective Ph.D. People will introduce us at parties as Doctor and Mister Martingale." I laughed, "Ho, ho!"

Dottie sat down abruptly. "I just can't believe this," she said.

"Think of Uncle Cyril," I pressed. "The old boy may never have another chance to go on his blessed expedition."

"Oh, shut up and let me think!"

I went into the kitchen and found her scotch. This one weakness had stayed with her: Cutty Sark. I poured ice and whiskey into two glasses and came back to the living room. I gave her one of the glasses.

"I can imagine how you must feel," I said, understandingly, "Just remember that you can call off the engagement anytime you want. I wouldn't want you to feel trapped."

She drank her drink and I made her another. She drank that too. In the middle of the third drink, she suddenly looked at me with her cool, academic eyes.

"All right, Luther, I'll do it."

"Rejoice! A kiss for the groom!" I stepped toward her. She waited till my face was approaching hers and then raised her glass and sipped it. I could have drunk from the other side of it. I nudged the glass with my lower lip, and felt the coldness of the ice.

"No, Luther," she hissed at me, "no unruly displays." She held up a slim, cool hand. I looked at it irritably. Oh,

well. I touched my lips to it. It tasted faintly of chalk.
Academic amore.

"I'll call Uncle Cyril now, and give him the good
news," she said, turning away toward the phone. I watched
her undulate away. If only I had the character to assault her!
A good rape might do her good. Some women were like
that. I tried to imagine what it would be like, but could not.
I wasn't the type. I liked my women to meet me halfway.
I went into the kitchen and made new drinks while Dot sat
down at her desk and began dialing.

* * *

We drove north from Boston to Weststock along Route 1.
Dr. Ashman was waiting for us in his office. It was the first
time I'd been there since my fateful interview with the
professor five years earlier. Things were a bit stiff; we eyed
each other for a moment. Then I stuck out my hand and
said, "How do you do, sir."

Automatically he extended his hand and I clasped it in
a firm grasp.

"Ummmph . . ." he replied. Behind his glasses, his eyes
were as blue and chill as I'd remembered them. I met his
gaze with candor, but with the expression of controlled dis-
comfort. I didn't want him to think I'd forgotten my sins,
but rather that I regretted them and had turned over a new
leaf.

Dottie helped out just then by stepping forward and
giving him a kiss on the cheek. He embraced her and then
held her at arms length, "Well, my dear, I understand that
you are to marry this young man."

She nodded, taking my arm, "That's right, Uncle Cyril."

The professor looked darkly at me.

"And we have other news for you," Dottie went on hurriedly. "Good news."

"I think I need a drink," said the professor tightly, "There's
a pub up the street with private rooms in the back. I have

some things to say that might be best said over scotch and water."

The weakness for scotch seemed to run in the family. "I understand, sir," I said, stepping back from the door. "Shall we go?"

He looked at me hard and went out the door. Dottie and I followed him half a block to the bar and joined him in a tiny cubicle in back. The waitress followed us in with her pad and pencil.

"J and B," said the professor. He looked at Dot, who modestly looked at me.

"Scotch, dear?" I asked, smiling down at her. She nodded, "Cutty Sark for the lady, then," I said to the waitress, "and a cup of black coffee for me, please."

The waitress went away, and I found the professor's eye upon me. "You aren't drinking, eh?"

"I don't drink, sir." I said, "I haven't had a drink in five years."

Dottie bowed her head, and her uncle looked hard at her. The waitress came back with their scotch and my coffee, and slapped paper doilies around in front of us. When she was gone again, the professor lit a cigarette and tasted his drink.

"Well, young man, I have already told Dottie this over the telephone, and I will tell you now: I do not approve of you, and I think of Dorothy here as my own daughter. I frankly cannot imagine why she has accepted your proposal, but I assure you that I oppose the engagement."

I sipped my coffee.

"Dottie and I have been corresponding regularly for five years, sir. And when I've been in Boston I've seen her. We love each other, and we know we can make a good life for ourselves."

"Doing what?" he asked. "I realize it's a bit old fashioned for me to ask, but how do you intend to support Dorothy?

Have you an occupation that can sustain you both? Who is your employer? What are your plans?"

"I do have plans, sir," I said firmly. "First, I plan to complete my college education." His eyes widened and then narrowed.

"I have hopes, sir, that you may help me return to Weststock."

"Have you indeed?" he replied coldly, leaning back. "I believe we discussed that possibility five years ago."

I brought up the reserve troops quickly.

"Dottie and I plan an October marriage," I said, "but before that, we will both enter college. She will be completing her course work for her Ph.D., as you know, and I'll be entering my junior year. If it proves impossible for me to enter Weststock, we will be going down to Florida where I've already been accepted for the fall term. I would prefer going to college here, as I'm sure you can understand, sir, because a transfer to Florida would mean that Dot's degree would probably be delayed. Her degree means a great deal to her, and to me."

I paused and sipped my coffee. I'd hit him fair. Her degree meant a lot to him, too. My lie about having been accepted at Florida wasn't hurting me a bit. The professor sat there and drew deeply on his cigarette.

"On the other hand," I went on, "if I could enter Weststock in the fall, Dot and I could get our degrees about the same time the year after next."

How he hated it! "If you could pass your courses, that is," he said, finally.

Both he and I knew why I'd flunked out, though, so that ploy meant nothing. I drank some more coffee. "Yes, sir," I said, "I'd have to do that, of course."

Uncle Cyril drank his scotch. "Hmmmph," he grunted. I nudged Dot with my elbow. She leaned forward and put her hand on his arm.

"Please, Uncle Cyril. Luther and I need your help. And, besides, I want you to give me away at the wedding!"

I hadn't heard that one before, but I gave Dot a loving glance and nodded sincerely.

"Harumph!" coughed Uncle Cyril. He fiddled with his glass. "Well . . ." He looked at Dottie, and the ice in his eyes melted a bit. I caught her glance, and nodded my head slightly. She put out a hand and closed it about his. "Uncle Cyril, there's something else . . . Something marvelous . . . Luther has a boat that he bought while he was working in Florida. . . ."

She drew the whole thing out for him, making pictures with words. She knew her uncle well, and catered both to his professional pragmatism and his private dream of finding the tomb. She balanced his ego against his brain, and showed him the whole thing: the boat, the two of us as crew, the bit of money I had, the vision of the Scandinavian coast, the whole works. The hook became embedded deeper and deeper while he played with the bait.

When Dottie's voice finally stopped, the professor's excitement was obvious. Still, he was suspicious.

"But why do you want to do this, young man? What good can it possibly be to you."

I set the hook. I looked at Dot proudly.

"It's a matter of scholarship, sir. I've never been a scholar, but this is my chance to make an original contribution."

He didn't even wriggle as I reeled him in.

CHAPTER 4

For an hour we sat and talked about the problems of the trip. . . . We needed passports, vaccinations, charts, and a hundred other things. The professor, full of careful enthusiasm, talked of his papers, his theories, and his chart. I sipped my coffee and wished I'd never decided to be a teetotaler. Finally the problems involving taking a small boat across the Atlantic came up, and I had an opportunity to dazzle both Dot and her uncle with my nautical lore, picked up mostly from two years on a Caribbean schooner that hauled tourists around the Islands. I spoke of drift, dead reckoning, prevailing winds, shooting the sun and stars, and other hogwash. The two of them seemed convinced.

The last thing Uncle Cyril did when we finally got up to leave was to accept my extended hand with a bit more vigor than the first time and say, "Young man, my position on the admissions committee is not one of complete influence, but I will do my best to have you readmitted for the fall term." He looked at his niece, "It is, I suppose, the least I can do for Dottie."

The old fraud. "Thank you, sir," I said warmly, "I'll mail in my formal request for re-entrance to the admissions office tomorrow."

Dottie gave him a daughterly hug and we walked him back to his office.

The next week passed hectically. I sent in my request for readmittance to Weststock, visited the Swedish and Danish Consuls for material on Scandinavia, and haunted the stores along and about Atlantic Avenue picking up supplies and provisions. Dot gave me a list from her uncle in which he'd named the gear he would need, and I tracked down as much as I could find. Finally my room at the hotel began to look like a small storehouse so I rented a pickup and trucked everything down to the boatyard where the *Gate of Horn* was moored.

I opened the hatches to let things air out and began to unload Wiglafson's personal gear. There was a 30.06 shark rifle slung over the main cabin door and a Luger pistol in a locker beside the captain's bunk; I didn't really want him to have those until after I'd sailed, so I kept them aboard. The rest of his gear, including half a case of that foul-looking black liquor he'd been drinking at the poker game, I packed into a couple of large cartons and put on shore. Then I spent the rest of the day listing everything still on board and packing in the supplies I had brought with me.

Finally, when everything below was in order, and Wiglafson's personal gear was loaded into the pickup, I shook out the sails and looked them over. They were heavy old-fashioned canvas, not new but stout and strong. Repairs had been made with good stitching. I could find no fault with either the working sails or the extra sets and spare canvas in the forward sail locker. Lashing the sails down onto their booms again, I climbed both masts and checked out the standing and running rigging. Everything was sound; Wiglafson had apparently liked his boat. Down on the deck again, I went over the fastenings, looked to the step of the mast and went over the tiller and rudder. Last, I got my face mask and swim suit and went over the side to check things out underneath. There was a touch of hair here and there, but it was apparent that she'd been hauled and painted not too long before. I got back on board, changed, locked the hatches and drove back to Boston. The *Gate of Horn* was ready even if I wasn't.

The problem was that I'd never really sailed a boat the size of the *Gate*. I'd worked little boats, day sailers, by myself, and I'd worked big boats in the Bahamas and the Islands as a crewman, but I'd never handled a boat over twenty-five feet by myself. Especially alone on the ocean. There is a lot of difference between piddling around the yacht club in a 220 or crewing on a Caribbean schooner during tourist cruises and being alone on the North Atlantic in a thirty-six-foot ketch. There are no friendly ports in the North Atlantic, and there are no rum swizzles or marimba bands to entertain the harbored voyager when the wind makes cruising rough. The prospect of spring storms distressed me, as did the matter of night sailing and that of navigation. I wasn't anxious to be run down by some freighter or fisherman during the night, and I was none too sure that my ability with a sextant was sufficient to keep me on course to the North Sea. I had many problems, and I brooded over them as I drove to Boston.

On Atlantic Avenue I stopped my pickup in front of the little café where Farrow and I and the others had had breakfast when Wiglafson had gone off to try and find money. I went in and saw George, the waiter, standing at the back near the kitchen door.

"Hello, George," I said.

He squinted at me.

"Hello, kid."

"You ever see Farrow around?"

"Maybe." He lit a cigarette.

"You know a big guy named Wiglafson?"

"Maybe I do."

"I've got some stuff of his. You think I could leave it here? I'm leaving town."

"What stuff?"

"Two boxes of gear that belongs to him. If you don't see him yourself, maybe you can tell Farrow the stuff's here and he can tell Wiglafson."

"We're kind of cluttered up as it is," he said, looking about the small room. I pulled out a bill. He looked at it and shook his head.

"Wiglafson might be wanting this stuff pretty bad," I said, still holding the bill.

A quick small smile quirked his lips for a second and was gone. "I'm pretty sure he might, kid. Okay, put your money away and bring the stuff in."

I got the boxes and brought them in. George gestured toward the end of the bar and I put them down there and stood up again.

"Any message?" asked George.

"Sure. Tell Wiglafson I brought this stuff down with me from Maine, and that I dropped it off before I went back."

Again the tiny smile touched his lips, "Okay, kid, I'll tell him. Anything else?"

"Yeah. Tell him I'll send his hardware to him in care of you after I get a little farther up the coast."

"I'll tell him that, too," said George. "Just make sure you take that hardware apart before you send it. I don't want no problems with the law."

"I'll send each piece in a separate box," I said, and walked out the door.

I left the pickup at the rental agency and went back to the hotel. The clerk lowered his paper long enough to see who I was. I was paid up, so he went back to his funnies and I went upstairs to call Dot. I'd had shots the day before, and both arms were sore from carting supplies from the room to the boat, so I was in need of solace. Besides, I wanted her to go over Uncle Cyril's mad expedition with me and help me get his rationale straight in my mind. Dot was in, and I conned her into feeding me some supper and sharing her scotch.

After showering and changing clothes, I went downstairs and out. The clerk had abandoned his comics and was talking to a little guy at his desk. He waved as I passed. I hoped the little guy would get a better room than I had, but I doubted if he would; it was not Boston's finest hotel.

I thought some more about the problem of sailing the boat alone as I walked across town to Dot's apartment. I thought I could probably do it, but I didn't relish the idea. The worst thing was that I couldn't raise the subject with either Dot or the professor; they might have ideas that would help, but they both thought that I was the master sailor. How our sins of pride catch up with us. In the end, maybe I could hire somebody, a college kid, maybe, who'd sailed the Bermuda races or something and wanted a ride to Europe.

I knocked at Dottie's door and met her with a confident smile and a fiancé-like embrace.

"Keep your hands to yourself," she said, catching my arms and pushing them back.

"Wait until the wedding, eh?"

"Something like that," she agreed, prim and tantalizing.

"We'll play it your way."

"I'm not playing. I'm not sure we're going to go through with this, but if we are, we're going to do it right. I'm not going to be your playmate of the year."

"Okay, okay." I mixed up a couple of drinks and touched my glass to hers, "Here, then, is a toast to chaste engagements and fertile marriages."

"Oh, don't talk that way, Luther. Take your drink out of the kitchen and sit down. We're having ham and beans for

supper and it'll be ready in just a minute. Someday I'd like
to have you come and see me just to talk to me. If I didn't
have a kitchen or bedroom, I don't think you'd ever come
over here at all."

It was woman's eternal complaint. She was probably
right, of course. Supper was delicious. I didn't mention
sex again, and we had a fine friendly meal. Afterward I
even offered to help with the dishes, and that made Dottie
even pleasanter, so that when we got back to the living
room all was well between us.

"Tell me about Uncle Cyril's project," I said, sitting across
from her. "I know he's got this notion that Beowulf was a
real man, but how did he get hung up on it? And what
makes him so sure he's right?"

She settled in her chair, "You know most of it already."

"Tell me again," I said. "There's something fascinating
about hearing the reasons one man has for thinking everybody is out of step but him."

She shrugged, "All right. I'll go over it again, if you want."
She leaned back and looked at the ceiling for a moment,
then peered at me from behind her glasses, "In the first
place, Uncle Cyril really isn't the only scholar who's wondered about the historicity of the hero of the *Beowulf* poem.
Most scholars have agreed, though, that the poem is essentially song rather than history, and that Beowulf probably
didn't really exist.

"I suppose Uncle Cyril really began to wonder about the
problem when he was still in graduate school. I think Wanley's note first roused his curiosity, because the note's description of the poem doesn't fit the poem as we now have
it. . . ." She paused, noting with classic academic satisfaction that I didn't know what she was talking about. Who the
hell was Wanley, after all? Did everybody know but me?

"I'll start from the beginning, Lute," said Dottie, with a

touch of that prissy scholastic smugness so characteristic, alas, of her family.

"Do that," I sighed. It was like being in the average college classroom: In order to possibly learn a little bit that was new, I had to hear again a great deal that was old. It is a standard fee that most teachers extract from their students: For an ounce of wisdom, you pay a pound of boredom. Still, in the long haul it wasn't a bad price. I lit a cigarette and got comfortable. Dottie collected her mental notes and put them in order. Then she began to lecture the class.

"Nobody knows who wrote the poem, or when, but many people believe that it must have first been written not earlier than the late seventh century and not later than the beginning of the ninth century.

"The poem as we now have it is based on a manuscript now in the British Museum. The name of the particular manuscript, or at least the name by which it's known, is *Cotton Vitellius, A. XV.* Everything we know about Beowulf is founded on that manuscript and a transcription made by Thorkelin.

"The manuscript *Cotton Vitellius,* now in the Museum, was made about the year 1000, two or three hundred years after the poem was originally composed. Two scribes made the copy in distinct scripts and spellings. Who commissioned the manuscript, who kept it, who saved it for the next six hundred years isn't really known; but sometime in the early seventeenth century, the manuscript entered the collection of Sir Robert Cotton, who died in 1631. The manuscript got its present name from its place in Cotton's library. Cotton had it placed under a bust of Vitellius which topped one section of his library shelves.

"In 1705, Humphrey Wanley, in his *Catalogue of Anglo-Saxon Manuscripts,* made the first known mention of the poem. In a note describing the poem, though, he represented it as being a narrative about Beowulf's and the Dane's wars against the Swedes. Anyone who's read the poem knows that it isn't about that at all. It's really about Beowulf's fights with Grendal, Grendal's mother, and the Fire Dragon. Uncle Cyril tells me that the discrepancy between Wanley's description of the poem in 1705 and our version of the poem in the 1800s and 1900s was what first interested him in the poem. But I'll get back to that later.

"Between 1712 and 1730, the Cotton library was housed in Essex House, but in 1730 the Government bought Ashburnham House in Westminster and moved the Cotton collection there for safekeeping. The next year, in 1731, there was a fire in Ashburnham House which destroyed a hundred manuscripts, injured nearly a hundred more, and burned most of the printed books in the collection. The *Beowulf* volume was badly scorched, and parts of the manuscript disintegrated before it could be correctly bound. Many words and several complete passages were lost as a result.

"Fortunately, the Danish scholar G. J. Thorkelin became interested in the manuscript and made a transcript of it in 1787, about fifty years after the fire. Later that year, he had a scribe make a second transcription of the manuscript. Thorkelin's own transcript is now called *Thorkelin A* and the other is *Thorkelin B*, in case you're taking notes, Luther."

I curled my lip, but I was listening.

"Home in Copenhagen," Dot went on, "Thorkelin spent several years preparing an edition of the poem. But then, in 1807, the English bombarded Copenhagen, and Thorkelin's house was burned and his edition of the poem burned with it. Fortunately, both transcripts of the poem survived the fire, and finally, in 1815, Thorkelin brought out the first printed edition of *Beowulf*. In 1837 the first English edition came out, and by 1900 dozens of translations had been made and dozens of scholars had written their opinions and interpretations.

"That more or less brings us up to date. The next thing to interest us is the box of manuscripts the college got hold of a few years ago. Uncle Cyril and others have been going over them, translating them from Old English and Latin into modern English. There are several kinds of writings in the manuscript collection, and most of them have nothing at all to do with *Beowulf*. Finally, though, when the poems and prose were initially straightened out and the men working on the manuscripts could really focus on particular things that interested them, Uncle Cyril discovered that one longish prose piece seemed to be about the fall of the Geats after Beowulf's death. The whole tale wasn't there, there were only fragments, but the writing contained references to the cairn where Beowulf was buried. . . ." She paused while I refilled our glasses from her dwindling supply of Cutty Sark.

"There was also this odd looking chart that he talks about in the journals. . . ." She paused again, and sighed. She was too intelligent to miss the implications about the chart bit. Any time somebody wants to hook some sucker on a treasure hunt, a secret chart is part of the package. Dot sipped her drink and arched her brows, "Everyone else thinks that both the chart and the prose fragments about the fall of the Geats are forgeries transcribed by somebody in the fourteenth century for purposes unknown to us. But Uncle Cyril thinks they're authentic tenth-century products, and that they can be related directly to a few key lines in the known version of *Beowulf*.

"You know the rest, I think. He thinks that Beowulf, or someone else who came to be called that in the poem, was a historic figure, and that he really lived, died, and was buried a thousand years or so ago. He thinks that he knows about where the burial cairn must have been; he's studied copies

of *Beowulf*, translations, the *Cotton Vitellius* manuscript
itself, and the chart and fragments in the manuscripts the
college has here, and he thinks he can find the burial.

"His problem has been getting money enough to prove
that he's right. If he can get to Sweden and find evidence
of the burial, he'll have solved one of the great riddles of
scholarship and will establish himself as the indisputable
leader in his field. That's why the whole thing is so important to him."

"Do you think he's right? That Beowulf's tomb really is
where he thinks it is?"

She shrugged, "I don't know. He's so convinced that he's
right that sometimes I can't help believing it too. I hope he
is. It would be marvelous if he really did find something. It
would be like finding Troy." She got up and went to her
bookshelves, and plucked a slim paperback from a shelf.
Seated again in her chair, she opened the book,

"Listen to this," she said, and began to read. I recognized
the passage. It was the description of the burial of Beowulf
after his battle with the fire-dragon.

> A huge heap of wood was ready,
> Hung around with helmets, and battle
> Shields, and shining mail shirts, all
> As Beowulf had asked. The bearers brought
> Their belovèd lord, their glorious king,
> And weeping laid him high on the wood.
> Then the warriors began to kindle that greatest
> Of funeral fires; smoke rose
> Above the flames, black and thick,
> And while the wind blew and the fire
> Roared they wept, and Beowulf's body
> Crumbled and was gone. . . .
> Then the Geats built a tower, as Beowulf
> Had asked, strong and tall, so sailors
> Could find it from far and wide; working

For ten long days they made his monument,
Sealed his ashes in walls as straight
And high as wise and willing hands
Could raise them. And the riches he and Wiglaf
Had won from the dragon, rings, necklaces,
Ancient hammered armor—all
The treasures they'd taken were left there, too,
Silver and jewels buried in the sandy
Ground, back in the earth, again
And forever hidden and useless to men.
And then twelve of the bravest Geats
Rode their horses around the tower
Telling their sorrow, telling stories
Of their dead king, and his greatness, his glory,
. . . .

Gold and jewels glittered in my mind. "I hope Uncle Cyril knows what he's talking about," I said.

"Well, he could very well be right. Even the most vocal disbeliever in Uncle Cyril's theory admits that there is a lot of known history in the *Beowulf* poem even if they don't accept Beowulf himself. The poem mentions characters and events—wars, fights, or what not—that are also mentioned by completely separate sources. . . ."

I'd done my homework, "You mean like Gregory of Tours. . . ."

She nodded, "Exactly. In the *Historia Francorum*, Gregory mentions the fatal trip Higlac made against the Franks. *Beowulf*, of course, tells us that Higlac was Beowulf's uncle and also tells of the unlucky expedition against the Franks. There is a good deal more too: The Swedish kings mentioned in the poem have correspondence with those in the *Ynglinga tal*, Higlac's raid against the Franks is mentioned in the *Liber Historiae Francorum*, the *Finnsburg Fragment* deals with the Finnsburg incident in *Beowulf*. As a matter of fact, it's almost impossible to really muster any concrete evidence that Beowulf didn't exist. The main reasons for disbelieving are linguistic or mythological. Beowulf's name is unusual, and both his name and his exploits are more understandable in terms of myth and folklore than of history. The poem itself is really almost the only written document we have that tells us anything at all about the life and times of that portion of the Dark Ages. Very few writings of any kind have come to us from that era. *Beowulf* is by far the most important of the manuscripts we do have, and if we didn't have it, we would really know very little at all of Scandanavia at that time. It's really quite a remarkable document."

"Monsters and dragons and all, eh?"

"Of course the monsters and dragons are the reasons no one will really accept the historicity of the poem, but several scholars have come up with explanations that are interesting. For instance, Uncle Cyril favors the notion that Grendal and his mother were possibly oversized cannibals who lived in some fen and who preyed on the Danes. There were cannibals in the region at that time, and for some time later, in fact. In Scotland as late as the seventeenth century, there were reports of cannibals living on the coast. . . ."

I lost her last words in the sound of heavy knocks on the door. Dottie looked up, "Who could that be?" She got up and went to the door. I slid my glass of scotch under the couch. If it was Uncle Cyril, I didn't want him seeing me off the wagon.

But it wasn't Uncle Cyril. When Dottie opened the door, a large hairy head poked in and looked at me. Then a huge hand brushed Dottie out of the way as if she were a doll, and Beorn Wiglafson came in, slamming the door behind him and knotting two hamlike fists.

Some shadow came with him, it seemed. He stood facing me from a darkness, and peered out at me with ancient fiery eyes. He was large and broad and sober, and he filled the room with an aura of age and strength.

"I have come for my boat," he said in a great grumbly voice. "Take me to it now, boy. I have no wish to stay longer in this city."

"Boat?" I said. "What boat?" When I stood up, my eyes were nearly on a level with his, but it was as though I were looking at a mountain.

"I will explain," said Wiglafson, and with his left hand he reached out and flicked me halfway across the room. "That boat," he rumbled.

"Hey!" Dottie shouted, "Hey, you! Stop that!" But Wiglafson paid her no mind and came toward me, his fists swinging like clubs at his sides.

CHAPTER 5

I was lucky. His first backhanded slap had rung my ears a bit, but hadn't done any real damage. Full of ham and beans and Cutty Sark, I wasn't really in fighting trim, though. When he swung again, I ducked away. I had the impression that he didn't really want to discuss the issue, so I hit him hard on the side of the jaw as he moved in. He turned and caught me backhanded again on the shoulder. Right on my vaccination! Pain! I scrambled to my feet and backed up, my arm throbbing. Somewhere I could hear Dottie's voice, high and frightened, but I had no time to understand her words. Wiglafson came toward me again, slowly and methodically.

I stepped in fast and hit him twice, then ducked his right and hit him again as I passed under his swinging arm. He turned after me, caught my shirt, and tore it off my back along with a bit of skin. Where was the damned door? I saw it behind him. He swung his left hand; it came like a hammer at my chest, but I was running backward and it only knocked me down. I scrambled behind Dot's desk, picked up her Weststock-emblemed captain's chair and threw it at Wiglafson's head.

It hit him fair, oiled oak thudding solidly against his skull. Blood appeared in his hair and he actually stopped in his tracks for a moment. But then his eyes seemed to brighten in a mad light, and he kicked the chair aside and reached down with both hands and tossed the desk on top of it. There was a splintering sound, and Dottie's papers filled the air. In the flurry of swirling paper I ran past him toward the door.

I was halfway there when his hand closed on my shoulder and spun me around. I swung hard as I was turned and succeeded in nearly breaking my fist on his forearm as his huge fist clubbed in at me. I didn't escape the punch, but I did deflect it enough so that it didn't kill me. The fist bounced my head back about six inches and changed my body into spaghetti. I flopped backward and sat down on the floor against Dot's bookcase. I watched Wiglafson walk across toward me and I managed to get up, but I knew the fight was over.

Then I saw Dottie coming up behind him. She had Shakespeare's bust in her hands, and as Wiglafson drew back his fist to finish me off, she lifted the bust and swung it, shattering it on the back of his head. Wiglafson held his punch and his knees caved a little. He shook his shaggy hair and his arms fell. Dottie still held the base of the bust in her hands, and she lifted it and broke that too on his head. Wiglafson's knees bent still farther, and his eyes drooped under their lids. He turned as if in a daze and swung his arms in a long arc toward the enemy behind him. His forearm hit Dot above her right ear and knocked her flat on her back. Her head bounced once on the carpet, and then no part of her moved.

Wiglafson looked dully down at her.

"By the gods," he muttered, "it is the girl."

He put a large hand to the back of his head and looked doubtfully at the large arm that had struck her. His knees seemed weak. I slithered behind him toward the table, which was still standing, for some reason, and looked for something heavy. Nothing was in sight, so I slid on into the kitchen. Dot's quart bottle of Cutty Sark sat there half full, and I picked it up regretfully and peeked back into the living room.

Wiglafson was on his knees looking at Dottie. ". . . Should not fight women . . ." he was saying in his grumbly voice. I tipped the bottle and took a long drink, then eased around behind Wiglafson and broke the quart of Cutty Sark right where Dottie had broken Shakespeare's bust. Wiglafson sighed and sat back on his heels. His face was blank. I pushed him on the shoulder and he toppled over on his side, stretched out his massive legs, and lay there. He seemed to be resting as much as anything else, as if he were just very tired. I would have preferred to have him unconscious, but there didn't seem to be any way to get him that way so I had to be content with things as they were.

I checked Dottie and found that she was still alive, picked her up and carried her into the bedroom. She moaned lowly as I put her down. At last I again had her defenseless and alone in bed. It was my big chance, I imagined, but neither of us was really in shape for it. I got a wet cloth from the bathroom and folded it across her brow. She was breathing evenly and looked fairly comfortable when I went back into the shattered living room. Wiglafson hadn't moved, so I straightened things up a bit while I did some fast thinking. By the time I got Dot's desk up on its own four legs again and had the remains of the captain's chair stacked on top of it I'd gotten an idea, so I got a glass of water from the bathroom and poured it on Wiglafson's head.

Then I sat down and watched him. His eyes blinked finally, and soon he sat up. There was blood in his hair and beard, and he found it on his hand after he'd rubbed his lumps for a while. Finally he got his eyes focused on me and seemed to remember what had been going on. I talked fast.

"Wiglafson, before you get up, I think we ought to discuss your boat. Now I admit that I do have it, and that maybe you do have some claim on it. But you did sign a witnessed bill of sale, and before you can get that boat back you'll have to go to court and prove that I won it from you in a poker game. Now both of us know that poker losses aren't legal debts in Massachusetts, but until you prove I got it illegally the boat is mine as far as the law is concerned."

He grunted and rubbed his head.

"What's more," I went on, "you've got a couple of other problems at the moment. You've broken into a girl's apartment and inflicted grievous harm on her and upon her guest, me. You can be put on trial for breaking and entering, assault and battery, disturbing the peace, and a dozen other things. You won't even get a chance to take your case against me to court until after you get out of jail for what you've done here today. By that time your boat could be long gone with me in it."

"You are not in it now, boy," he noted, pulling his legs under him.

"That's right," I agreed hurriedly. Like a fool I'd left him between me and the door. "But that brings me to my point. I know where the boat is, right? I've got a claim that may or may not stand up in court, but will sure as hell stand up until then, right? You want the boat back, but if you try to muscle me for it, I'll slap charges on you that will keep you in court for months, right?" I leaned forward and looked him in the eye, "Now, what would you say if I offered you a deal that not only gets you off the hook for your little celebration here but would give you your boat back with no argument?"

He looked up at me with his ancient suspicious eyes. "I would say for you to talk some more."

"All right, here's what I have in mind. You work with me

for this summer on your boat, and in the fall the boat will be yours again with no argument from me. I'll give you the bill of sale you signed, the boat's papers and any claim on them I might have, and a waiver clearing you of any responsibility for what's just happened here. Now think carefully; I do have some sort of claim on your boat, and even if I don't I might be able to keep it for a long time anyway. On top of that, legal or not, you did lose a lot of money to me in that poker game. By working for me this one summer you'll be free from all debt to me. You'll owe me nothing."

"My lawyer says I owe you nothing now."

"Gaming debts are matters of honor, not of law," I said. It was not as weak a thrust as it might seem; honor has gotten more people in and out of trouble than reason ever did.

"That is so." He rubbed his bristling beard.

"We can settle the thing honorably between us then," I hurried on. In the bedroom I could hear noises as Dottie stirred around, and I wanted to settle this thing before she woke up and started asking questions.

Wiglafson grunted. "What is this work that I shall do? Poppies? Guns?"

"Nothing like that. All I want you to do is help me sail the *Gate of Horn* to Sweden and then spend the summer digging, maybe, somewhere along the coast."

"Ah." His ageless eyes brightened slightly, "That is my homeland. I know that coast."

I smiled happily, "You don't say? Then you should be really interested in our summer plans. . . ." I outlined the project quickly, for Dottie was moaning a bit now, and was squeaking around on the bed. "The professor, Dr. Ashman, is the only one who knows exactly where we'll be going or what we'll be doing," I concluded. "Well, how does it sound to you? Do we have a deal?"

He thought for a while, thinking, probably, that since we were really only going where he wanted to go anyway, he might as well agree. Then he nodded his head, "Yes, I will do it."

I put out my hand and he enclosed it in his great fist.

"Gently on the fingers, please," I cautioned. He laughed and rolled up onto his feet, looking around the room.

"We have some good fight here, ya?"

"Yes, we did."

"Yes, you did," said Dottie from the doorway of her bedroom. She was sagged against the casing holding the wet cloth to her head. "Luther Martingale, who is this man? What's he doing here? My God, look at the mess!"

"Dottie, this is my first mate and old buddy, Beorn Wiglafson. Beorn, this is my fiancée, Dottie Ashman."

"We've met," said Dot, and she wavered into the room and sat down on the couch.

Beorn was looking at her with an expression of infinite regret, "Ah," he rumbled, "the woman. The lady who came from behind." His voice softened, "Lady, when I struck I did not know who was there. It is not right that a man strike a woman so. Would that my blow had fallen on empty air, and that you were not hurt." He raised his giant hands in a gesture of monstrous regret, and his eyes rested on her with a curious, sad light.

"I'll live, thank you," said Dot, looking at him with dazed curiosity. "It was my own fault. I should have ducked but I never thought you would be able to turn like that."

"Oh," he smiled. "You struck good blows, lady, but for one such as me, many such blows are needed. Still, I was half blind; had I seen clearly that so fair a woman as you had struck me, I would have stopped my blow."

The two of them were looking at each other with chagrined wonder, and Dottie actually colored a bit. Then she seemed to pale slightly.

"Gentlemen, if you will excuse me, I think I'll go into the bathroom and throw up my supper." She got to her feet and disappeared into the bath. Sick sounds preceded the noise of running water.

"By the gods; I hope she is not greatly harmed," grumbled Beorn, looking at the closed bathroom door.

"She may be," I said sternly, sure that she wasn't, but seeing no harm in emphasizing Beorn's dependence on me to keep him out of jail. I was feeling pretty slushy myself, but I wasn't about to show it in front of Beorn, who gave no sign at all of similar trouble, so I changed the subject.

"How in the world did you find me here, anyway?"

"Ah, it was a simple thing. I hire a little lawyer to help me; then I go to Gloucester to find the boat. I look there and in harbors down the coast for three days, but of course she is not there." He chuckled, "Then I come back to Boston and find my little lawyer again and maybe hire a flying ma-chine—a helicopter, you know—to fly about and look down for my boat. But money is scarce; I have only the small bag of gold coin. So the lawyer hires a policeman—a searcher—and he goes to hotels and bars to find you. Today he finds your hotel and sees you when you go out. The clerk tells him it is you, and he follows you to this place. When you do not come out of these rooms, he uses the telephone and calls my lawyer who calls me. I come to find you." He spread his hands, "It was a simple thing."

"I guess so," I agreed. Simple for him; simple-minded of me.

Still, things were really going along well. I had some lumps and bruises, and had lost part of my shirt, but I had something more important: a man who knew the *Gate of Horn* and could sail her on the high seas, and who, even better, knew the Swedish coast. The gods were smiling upon me with amazing grace. I could almost see my inheritance check lying in its little gold pot at the end of Aunt Delia's rainbow.

"One more thing," I said. "Dottie and the professor don't know anything about how I got my hands on your boat. They think I got it by hard work, and I want them to keep on thinking just that, understand?"

He blinked his old eyes at me and then nodded, "Good. It does not matter to me. In the end, the boat will be mine anyway."

"That's right, Beorn," I smiled. The finality of his tone was disturbing.

The bathroom door opened and Dottie, face scrubbed and hair brushed, came out to join us.

"Ah," mumbled Beorn. "You look well, lady." She had a red and blue mark high on her right forehead where his arm had bruised her, but she did look much better.

"Gee, I'm sorry, Dot," I said, "but when old Beorn here came in, thinking this was my room we just forgot ourselves and started rough-housing a bit. We're sorry as hell that we wrecked your place. We'll get you a new Shakespeare and a new chair as soon as we can, and we'll help you straighten things out some more before we go."

She surveyed the mess. "Never mind. You two have helped enough already. I must say that I never heard of two grown men greeting each other in quite this fashion."

"Ho! ho!" I laughed, giving Beorn's unbudging shoulder a comradelike jab with my aching fist. "Old Beorn and I have scared the daylights out of half the bars on Bimini with these meetings; right, Beorn?"

"Ya," said Beorn stolidly, "I guess so."

"This was a little more boisterous than usual, I'll admit," I went on, "but we haven't seen each other in quite a while. I'm sure sorry we messed up your apartment, Dot, but I just forgot myself."

"My head aches," she said. "I guess I've outgrown the

games boys play. Why don't you two leave and let me get some beauty sleep. I feel like I need it."

"You have no need of such sleep, lady," said Beorn, "but we will go, yes?" He looked at me.

"Sure." I got my coat from the closet and put it on over the shreds of my shirt.

"I'll call you later, Dot," I said at the door.

"Good night, lady," said Beorn, filling the doorway with his bulk.

"Good night," she answered. She looked at Beorn and frowned at the sight of the dried blood in his hair. "Before you go, I think I should wash off some of that blood, at least."

He touched his head with his great hand. "This?" He chuckled, "It is nothing. The sting of a bee; no more."

"Ah. Good night, then."

As we went down the stairs I looked back and saw her standing in the doorway watching us go.

Beorn and I worked hard all the following week. Uncle Cyril, unable to escape the rigors of his teaching schedule, sent fretful notes and telephone calls down to us from Weststock. There were thousands of things to get, it seemed. Besides shovels, picks, buckets to haul dirt and strainers to sift it, we needed stores for four people, insect repellent, and countless other items I never would have thought of. Beorn proved a great deal better at collecting obscure items of equipment than I was. He knew Boston well.

"I sail in here many times," he explained. "Is a fine harbor, and I know good people like Farrow to have fine time."

Beorn had gotten his gear from the café and stowed it back on board the boat. Uncle Cyril was sputtering like a sick hornet, trying to keep track of everything. I saw Dot almost every night, but she was busy with schoolwork too, and coolly declined my occasional hints that I stay for the night. We spent a good deal of time talking about the trip Beorn and I would be taking across the Atlantic, and I calmed her fears of the hazards of the voyage by my exaggerated tales of my experience on the high seas and repeated assurances of our boat's seaworthiness. Almost as much time was spent talking about Beorn. She was fascinated by him.

"He's such a brute," she mused. "I never knew anybody like him."

"You've called me a brute too, remember."

She sniffed, "It's not the same thing, Lute."

The day came when we actually had everything, or nearly everything we needed. That night Beorn and I went to Dot's apartment for supper with her and Uncle Cyril. Dot let us in and gave Beorn a glass of scotch and me a cup of black coffee. I looked at it with disgust, but sipped it nevertheless. A bit later Uncle Cyril arrived, looking haggard but enthusiastic. He and Beorn had taken great fancies to each other, the professor by Beorn's mass, and Beorn by the professor's occupation and intellect. They greeted each other like old friends. An odd pair: The professor, ascetic, thin, intellectual; and Beorn, massive, ageless, and weathered by sea living.

After the meal, we talked of meeting in Denmark.

"Dottie and I will leave Boston on June seventh, the day after commencement," the professor said, smoking his umteenth cigarette. "We'll meet you in Copenhagen on June tenth." He looked at Beorn and me, "That gives you almost two months to get the boat over there. Will you have time?"

"Ya," said Beorn. "The *Gate of Horn* is not fast, but she will take us there in time. She has crossed this sea before."

"Excellent." The professor dug into his pocket and

brought out an envelope. He gave it to me, "Here is a list of equipment and supplies we can get in Copenhagen when we get there. If you get in a few days early, the two of you can buy these things and get them on board before Dot and I arrive. That way we can save time and get started toward Sweden without delay."

"Very good, sir." I put the envelope in my pocket. I hoped the list wasn't too long, because my money was getting pretty damned low. I had a couple of thousand dollars in the operation already.

"I have one more thing to give you," said the professor, reaching into another pocket. He drew out two paperback books, and gave one to Beorn and one to me. "Those are copies of a translation of *Beowulf*," he said, "I thought you might like to have them. They may give you something to think about on the voyage over. You'll probably have plenty of time to read, and if you'll pay especial attention to the final pages of this book, you may have a better understanding of why this expedition is so important to all of us."

"Thank you very much, sir," I said. I'd read the poem a hundred times already, and had a good deal of it memorized. Beorn, on the other hand, seemed sincerely impressed with the little book. He held it in his massive hand as if he held a diamond.

"It is the story of a great hero," said Uncle Cyril. "This book tells of his life and death. It is my hope that we will find the place where his followers buried him." He leaned forward, "For two hundred years people have thought that the hero, *Beowulf*, was not a real man, but was a fiction made up by bards in the days before writing. But I am sure he was real; and if we can find his tomb, or evidence of it, we will astound the world and change the thinking of many people. It would be a great discovery!"

Beorn nodded his great head. His face was oddly enigmatic. "I will read the book when we sail. When we see you again, I will talk of it to you some more, professor."

"Good, Beorn."

Across from him, Dottie watched Beorn as he slid the book carefully into one of his pockets. She'd never met anyone like him. Neither had I, for that matter. He reminded me most of all of some Indians I saw once on the coast of Mexico. They were squat, lean men who'd come out of the back country to trade for salt. They stayed just long enough to barter and then disappeared inland again without letting anyone know just who they were or where they'd come from. The storekeeper who'd traded his salt for their goods shrugged when I asked about them.

"They come from the mountains," he'd said simply. "They are of the old people." He'd reached behind his counter and brought out a small leather purse and opened it. "They bring these in trade. I sell them to tourists." He reached into the bag and brought out an object and put it on the counter. It was a carved piece of jade with threads of gold inlaid in it. "I do not know where they get the stone," he said. "There is no such stone in this state."

Beorn was like those Indians to me: of some time and place I knew nothing of.

It was late when Beorn and I got up to leave the apartment. We were bunking on the *Gate of Horn* that night and were catching the tide out of the harbor in the morning. In front of Uncle Cyril where she could make no evasive action or comment, I gave Dot a chaste kiss. Her lips were cool. Beorn watched.

"I'll cancel my classes for tomorrow morning, and come down with Dottie to see you off," said the professor.

We said our goodnights, and Beorn and I went down into the somber Boston night.

"You have a good woman," said Beorn, pulling a stained clay pipe from a pocket and lighting it as we walked down

Beacon Street. "Thoughts of her will make your voyage short."

If only it were true. Still, I nodded as if in agreement. "A good woman is hard to find," I said.

"Ya," said Beorn, "is true."

I wondered what was going on inside his shaggy head.

By the time Dot and the professor arrived the next morning, Beorn and I had been up at work long since. We'd filled the water tanks, checked hatches and fastenings, and secured everything below and on deck. Out in the harbor the wind was beginning to lift the fog.

"A good day for sailing," grinned Beorn to the professor. "Come. We go below."

Dot had a camera, which she gave to me as we followed the others into the cabin. "Here. Take a lot of pictures. I want a photographic record of this whole expedition. Uncle Cyril hopes to get a book out, and if he does, pictures will help a lot."

In the cabin, Beorn dug into his locker and produced one of his dreadful black bottles of liquor.

"We drink to a successful voyage," he said, getting out glasses and passing them around.

"None for me," I said. I had a case of scotch under my bunk, but what Uncle Cyril didn't know wouldn't hurt me.

"Is necessary to drink," said Beorn firmly. "Before a sea voyage all men who sail drink to the sea."

"Water, then."

"Water is not the custom," said Beorn insistently.

"Oh, Luther," said Dot, flashing a quick look at her uncle, "do make an exception this one time."

"Certainly, my boy," chimed in the professor, who was in excited good humor. "Take just a drop to gain the propensity of the gods."

"Well . . ." I hummed a moment and then gave in and

watched with delight as Beorn sloshed my glass nearly full.

"There," he boomed, "a drink for a man!" He lifted his glass. "My people call it the Whale's Road. So we drink to that, ya? To the whale's road, to fair winds, and to our strong ship!"

We drank. The liquor was strong and rich. We looked at it, impressed.

We drank to a successful expedition, to Beorn and me, the mighty sailors, and then to the sea again. Then Beorn capped the bottle and put it back in the locker.

"One glass is enough," he said with a great-toothed grin. "More than one makes a man slow to move."

"Where is your radio?" asked Dot, looking about.

"No radio," I said.

"Radio, pah!" snorted Beorn, "what for we need one? The sea and the sky will tell us what we need to know of the weather. A radio is good only for noise."

Dot frowned, and Beorn leaned across toward her. "Ah, do not be alarmed, lady. We have compass and sextant and charts." He touched his forehead and then his massive chest, "I know things here and here."

I looked at my watch. "Time to go," I said.

"Oh, dear," sighed Dot. "Well, Uncle Cyril, let's get out of their way."

On the dock I shook hands with the professor and gave him a hearty "See you soon, sir." Then I went to Dot and, since this was my last chance, and since Uncle Cyril's presence once more prevented any open resistance on her part, I gave her a long lover's kiss and a few fiancé-like fondles. She got hold of my hand finally and disengaged herself enough to step back.

"Goodby, dear," she said through gritted, grinning teeth.

"I'll be thinking of you," I smiled in return.

On board, Beorn started the engine, and the *Gate of Horn*

trembled into life. I went forward to the bowline and cast it free. The tide swung the bow slowly away from the dock. Beorn loosed the stern line and took the tiller.

"Goodby, goodby," we all called as the boat slid in a wide arc out from the landing. Beyond the breakwater, Beorn brought the boat into the wind and we broke out the sails. Then, as we fell off toward the sea, he cut the engine and we slacked off the sheets to catch the offshore wind and watched the canvas fill.

Far to our left the Boston skyline loomed indistinctly in the city smoke and still rising fog. We came to the President Roads and turned due east. Somewhere a bell buoy was droning, and far, far behind us, tiny on a distant dock, Dot and the professor still stood, watching us as the wind and tide carried us out toward the sea.

As we cleared Ceer Island, I was opening the first bottle from my case of Cutty Sark.

CHAPTER 6

For days the wind held from the southwest and we rode before it with scarcely a change in the setting of the sails. We stood watches at night, and moved north out of the steamer routes as we left Boston behind. At night we could sometimes see the lights of passing ships coming in from Europe, and once the *Shalom*, of Israel, passed in the afternoon less than half a mile from us. Through our glasses I watched the passengers on deck leaning on the rail watching us through their glasses, and I waved and received a hundred waves in return.

It grew cold as we moved north and the wind became more variable. I shot our position every day and wrote it down in the log I was keeping. Beorn didn't carry a log; "Is much bother," he said. "I know where I come and where I go and what I do. You write if you wish." So I did; I wrote things down and took photos of Beorn and, with the aid of a delayed shutter device, of myself doing various things around the boat. I let my beard grow, so by the time we were a couple of weeks out I looked properly adventuresome.

Beorn had the sea in his blood; he could tell when the waves would mount and when they would calm, and would often reset the sails long before I saw any need for doing it. And he was always right. If he reefed sail, the wind rose within an hour and blew hard; and often he was out removing the reefs even as the wind died down again. Sometimes he would set the sheets and go below to read the book the professor had given him, saying, "There. Is all right for three, four hours. You tie tiller if you want." At first I dared not leave the helm, but always Beorn was right: for three or four hours the boat would sail without effort; at the end of that time Beorn would come back on deck, look around at the sky and sea, and reset the sails. Finally, I did begin tying the tiller and either reading from the dozen books I'd brought or studying the charts of the Swedish coast that I'd bought in Boston.

"Beorn," I said one morning, as we heeled along through a quartering sea drinking coffee laced with scotch, "how do you do it? How the hell do you know these things before they happen?"

He shrugged and laughed, "I do not know, Luther. I have always been on the sea, and I have always known these things. My father was of the sea also. Along the coast they called him Silkie, for he seemed to the landsmen there to be more seal than man. He too knew the wind and the waters, and perhaps it is from him that I know these things. When I was young, my father told me that my mother was not of the sea, but of the land, and that I am of both. It may be true, but I think I am more of my father than of my mother."

"Your father was a seaman, too, then."

"Of course. My father and his father and his father. We have been seamen for many generations. There was a time, I think, when we were not, when we were of the land, but that was long ago. There was a feud between peoples then, I was told when I was young, and my people lost a mighty battle and took to their boats. My uncle sang songs of that time to me when I was a boy sailing with him and my father. He was a great singer and knew the old songs well, but I am no singer and have forgotten many of the words." He gestured toward the cabin, "The little book that the professor gave me. That book is like the songs my uncle sang. My uncle would have liked that book, I think. I am happy reading it."

"Your uncle sang stuff like that when you were a boy? When was that?"

"Long ago. I do not count winters. It was long ago."

"Is your uncle still alive? Does he still sing those songs?"

"Alive? Ah, no. My uncles and my father are long dead now. They were large men in their time, but they have passed now. My uncle sailed his ship on a voyage and did not return to my aunt or my cousins. And now my aunt too has passed, and only my cousins remain."

"Too bad," I said, "I'd have liked to hear your uncle's songs."

"It can be done still," rumbled Beorn, "for I have a cousin who is a singer. His woman and his daughters live on his farm south of Göteborg. But you will not see him this summer, for he is sailing and will not be back before midwinter, I think."

"Where did he go?"

"East. There are ports in the East where my people go for trading. It is his first trip there, and his daughters were small when he left." He nodded contentedly. "My brother, Sigemund, sails with him, I hear."

"How old is your brother?" I could not tell how old Beorn was. There was a look of great age about him, but in looking closely at him I could find no particular sign that he was any age in particular. The only thing I was sure of was that he was not young.

In answer to my question, he shook his head, "I cannot say how old he is. We were children together on the boats of my father and uncle and then we had boats of our own."

He heaved his massive shoulders, "It is of little difference. We are men, and we go men's ways across the earth." Looking off to starboard then, he said, "It is time to haul in the sheets, Luther. The wind is shifting to the southeast."

That ended my questions, and I went forward and began adjusting lines on the foresails. A few minutes later the wind turned, but we were ready for it and drove on close hauled, the spray from the *Gate of Horn*'s blunt bow flying sharply back into our faces.

I had never been so far from land before. Always in the Caribbean there had been islands or land masses somewhere in sight or just beyond the curve of the ocean; but out here there was nothing but water for thousands of miles in front of us. Somewhere to the north, Greenland lay in spring ice, and America daily fell farther behind. The sky and sea changed color from blue to gray to black to green and back to blue, with shades of color swirling into patterns and then other patterns. The swells and waves came endlessly from the horizon and rolled endlessly under and past us toward the other side of the world. I wondered at times how small we must appear to the sea birds that sometimes still floated in the high sky above us.

There was a loneliness to it that was rooted in the fact of our total isolation on a plane of curved blue that reached from hemisphere to hemisphere. Nothing save our dot of a boat was on that plane, it seemed, and the plane was so vast that we would never reach its rim. We sailed for days and weeks and yet, had I not shot the sun and stars and thus verified our movement, we might well have been bobbing in one spot; nothing indicated movement or progress. I began, for the first time, to have some grasp of the peculiar strength and madness that sets the sailor of small boats apart from other travelers of the oceans. Only a man of a certain character could or would go to sea alone as Beorn or Slocum or Pidgean had done. Theirs was a mystic strength that isolated them from their fellows and, in part, from me as well.

About two weeks out, the sky cleared and the wind died away. For a while we caught imprecise little breezes from all points and managed, by constant resettings of the sails, to inch along for a few miles. Then even Beorn gave up the effort to catch a wind, and we settled back and watched the sails hang limp from their gaffs. We bobbed on the water to the sound of slapping lines and the soft sighs of mild rolling swells lifting the boat and dropping it. The wind was gone and we lay becalmed under a setting sun. That night the air was cold and dry. After supper, when we tossed our leavings overboard, crumbs bobbed alongside the hull, rising and falling in perfect cadence with the boat.

For three days we got scarcely a breeze, and all that time the currents turned us and moved us silently back toward the west away from Europe. Beorn read his *Beowulf*, his eyes slowly crossing the lines as he got them into his mind. He was the slowest reader I ever saw, but certainly the most persistent. The pages of his book turned slowly in his massive hands, and his ancient, patient eyes plodded from word to word. Sometimes he would stop reading and seem to reach into his memory for some recollection which would add to the substance of the writing before him.

Less patient, I zipped through the poem two or three times, concentrating on the tale of the dragon:

Afterwards, in the time when Higlac was dead
And Herdred, his son, who'd ruled the Geats
After his father, had followed him into darkness—
Killed in battle with the Swedes, who smashed
His shield, cut through the soldiers surrounding
Their king—then, when Higd's one son
Was gone, Beowulf ruled in Geatland,
Took the throne he'd refused, once,
And held it long and well. He was old

With years and wisdom, fifty winters
A king, when a dragon awoke from its darkness
And dreams and brought terror to his people. The beast
Had slept in a huge stone tower, with a hidden
Path beneath; a man stumbled on
The entrance, went in, discovered the ancient
Treasure, the pagan jewels and gold
The dragon had been guarding, and dazzled and greedy
Stole a gem-studded cup, and fled.
But now the dragon hid nothing, neither
The theft nor itself; it swept through the darkness,
And all Geatland knew its anger . . .

I knew Aunt Delia's gold was real, and I wondered if
Uncle Cyril's was. Once, while I stared broodingly into the
depths of the water, a trio of great dark shapes passed under
the boat, huge and dark and indistinct in the cold, ageless
sea, and disappeared into the vastness from which they had
come; larger than elephants, larger than whales, monstrous
and formless, they undulated through the blue-black depths
of the cold Atlantic with swan-necked grace and were gone
before I could even cry out for Beorn.

"There are things in the sea," he agreed casually, when I
called him on deck.

I shot the sun and muttered curses at the currents that
floated us backward, away from Sweden and Beowulf's
gold, if any. I whistled for a wind and got out my charts and
went over them again. If the professor was right, Beowulf's
tomb stood high on a hill somewhere along the ragged western coast of Sweden. There was a lot of coast, and I hoped
that Uncle Cyril knew more about where to look than I did.
Without a fairly sure knowledge of where to look, a man,
or even an army of men could spend years going in and out
of inlets or climbing coastal hills.

If the tomb existed, no one had found it in a thousand
years, so it was not going to be easy for us either. I decided

to ape Beorn's patience. I sipped scotch, nibbled on biscuits and jam, and tried to forget our westward drift. I read my books, wrote in my log, which was becoming more of a journal, and thought a good deal about Dottie. In my mind she took full form and tempted me with her fine lines and cold mind. Beorn would look up at me sometimes in those moments and seem to look into my brain.

I was surprised that I thought so much about Dottie. On board the Caribbean schooners there were usually a good many single or separated secretaries from New York or Cleveland or whatnot who'd saved their pennies for a week of romantic island-hopping, so I'd not suffered any dearth of female companionship. In fact, it had gotten to the point, finally, when the departure of those moon-eyed young women was as welcome as their arrival; such girls are nice for a while, but after a bit can get to be a weight around the neck.

Alone in the middle of the Atlantic, things were different; I had only memory to keep me company. I began to imagine what life would be like if Dot and I married and settled down. A man needs a woman, I decided.

"Ya," rumbled Beorn, "it is true."

"What?" I asked, starting up from my charts and coming out of my daydreaming. Beorn sat at the tiller puffing his old clay pipe and looking out across the windless water with ancient eyes. The *Gate of Horn* rolled gently as the sea passed beneath her and inched her toward the west.

"I say that it is true what you say," said Beorn, "a man does need a woman. She should be at his home when he returns from the sea. Without such a woman a voyage does not really end, Luther; but when a woman does wait for you, you may go ashore with contentment until it is time to sail again. Such a woman is needed, I think."

"I was thinking of Dottie," I said.

"Ya. She is a good woman for a man to have." He nodded

his shaggy head, his great beard moving across his dark sweater, "When you see her in Köbenhavn, it will be a good thing. She is strong, fit for bearing sons and daughters, and she is of a good mind like the professor.

▶ "It is well for a woman to be of such a mind, for when her man is at sea or working at his farms, she will not be tricked by wanderers or lose her farm to usurers. She will welcome her man to a home that is better than it was when he left it, and will show a profit on his crops and cattle. His children will be straight and will honor him and give him comfort." He looked at me, "When a man is at sea, it is good that he should know that his woman waits for him. It is a comfort to think of her, and to know that she thinks of him. Such thoughts make long voyages short and bring winds that drive the ship home."

"Have you a wife, then?" I wasn't too damned sure that cool Dottie Ashman was prepared to live on a farm somewhere while I sailed the seven seas.

"My woman is passed," said Beorn without emotion. "She bore me a daughter and a son and kept a good house for me. But then she passed away from me during a hard winter. We had a good life together."

"What about your children?"

His eyes brightened, "Ah! My son is sailing with Lars Grenmere. Soon he will have his own ship. My daughter lives with my brother's wife. Soon she will take a husband. Good men live where my brother lives, and my daughter is near the age of marriage."

"What about you, Beorn? Will you marry again?"

He nodded his head, "Ya. My father had three wives, and it is right that I should take another woman. I have been without one for many years now, and it is time for me to marry again."

"I suppose so," I said, thinking ahead to fall. "I'm getting married myself, you know."

"Ya. I have been told of your plan." He swept the horizon with his eyes, and his voice and eyes were without expression when he spoke. Then without hurry he raised his arm and pointed to the southeast.

"Look there, Luther."

At the edge of the horizon a small cloud hung high in the air. Beneath it and behind it the water was dark.

"Wind comes," said Beorn. "Soon we shall be underway."

"Are the sails okay?"

"They are fine for now," said Beorn, but his mind really seemed to be on something else.

The cloud advanced and passed to our right, obscuring the sun for a moment, and the first breath of wind touched the sails. The *Gate of Horn* began to move. The wind increased and the sails filled and we were underway again. I thought of Dottie and imagined her waiting for me on the docks of Copenhagen. Beorn's eyes were roaming the rigging, and whatever thoughts he had lay deep within his hairy skull. To the southeast, clouds were building across the sky, making castles and dragons in the sky.

> Then they sailed, set their ship
> Out on the waves. . . .
> Ready for what came they wound through the currents,
> . . . . and were borne
> In the lap of their shining ship, lined
> With gleaming armor, going safely
> In that oak-hard boat to where their hearts took them.
> The wind hurried them over the waves,
> The ship foamed through the sea like a bird. . . .

By midnight the wind was high and both of us were on deck taking in sail. The water was black and cold, and the waves were rising. Spray and scud flashed white all around us, and foam flew across the decks when the *Gate of Horn*'s blunt bow dipped and dug into the water. The wind was bitter cold and the footing on deck was treacherous as we moved fore and aft securing lines and canvas. There was water in the cockpit when I took the tiller to stand my watch.

"I fix coffee," Beorn said, going below. Cold and miserable, I puffed on a wet cigarette and watched the compass and rigging, keeping us pounding along roughly on course. Beorn brought the coffee on deck. He had laced it with the dark liquor he kept in his locker, and almost immediately a warmth began to build out from my belly.

"Good stuff!" I yelled at him across the wind.

His teeth gleamed in the binnacle light, "Ya, you drink and you will not be cold. I go below now and sleep for a bit."

Through the half-opened hatch I watched him lay his great bulk on the bunk and pull a blanket around him. He seemed to sleep immediately, and I wondered how he could do it in the midst of such a storm. But soon I was too busy to think of him any more, for the waves climbed higher and higher until I stopped looking at them and could see only the thrashing boat.

Two hours later, it was obvious that we'd have to drop more sail. I yelled down to Beorn and he came up immediately, clear-eyed and calm. Between us we got the boat balanced between stern jib and full-reefed mizzen, and the *Gate of Horn* rode easier. Beorn went below again and returned instantly to sleep. In the early dawn he awoke, fixed hot mush and laced coffee for our breakfast and took over the tiller. Then I went to my bunk in the cold, gray morning light and let the ache in my bones drive me into an uncomfortable sleep.

When I woke, the boat was going smoothly and sunlight was streaming through the portholes. Looking out, I saw blue sky and rolling waves coming from the beam. I glanced at my watch and saw that I'd been asleep ten hours! I ducked up into the cockpit and found Beorn relaxing at the tiller munching crackers.

"Ah, Luther. It is a fine day."

"Why the hell didn't you get me up for my watch?"

He raised a weathered hand, "What need. You had seen us through the night. Now the sea is fine and running, and old Beorn likes to sail on such a day. So I let you sleep, ya?"

I sat down and ate a cracker. The *Gate of Horn* was drumming along under full sail, heeled to port and rolling eastward.

"Any damage?" I asked, looking aloft.

"Damage? No. A small storm like that will do no harm to this vessel if she is under a hand as good as yours, Luther."

A small storm, eh? Still I was flattered by his comment.

"It is only necessary to keep the sails balanced," said Beorn. "With balanced sails the *Gate of Horn* will sail in almost any sea."

"Almost?"

"Ah, my friend, any boat will go down if the sea wishes it so. There is no vessel which is so strong as the sea. There are times when one must run away if he can and wait for the water to become less angry. One must not think that he is mightier than the oceans, for no man is as mighty as that." The note of caution left his voice, "Still, a man and boat are strong and need not fear the sea. They need only to know it and themselves to be safe on the waters, ya?"

"I'll take your word for it," I said. "In the western part of the United States they have a saying about men and horses. They say: 'There's never a horse that's never been rode, and never a man who's never been throwed.'"

Beorn nodded, "It is the same wisdom, I think."

The difference was that when you got thrown from a horse you landed on solid ground and stood a chance of walking home. Out here the walking was difficult.

CHAPTER 7

For days we sailed on into prevailing southeasterlies.
We saw two planes high to the south of us with the sunlight
glinting on their wings, and once had a slow moving sub-
marine spotter come down from the north, circle us twice,
then dip its wings in salute and pass on to the south; but we
saw no boats.

For a week then we had variable winds and some heavy
rain laced with snow, but afterward the wind swung to the
southwest and we sailed free in front of it without changing
sail. We were making good time, if my sextant work was
accurate, and would be in Copenhagen well before the tenth
of June. I was beginning to feel better about everything.
The only thing I might have asked for was warmer air, for
the winds were constantly cool and often cold and raw. The
month of May might bring flowers to the land but it brought
only chills to the *Gate of Horn*. Beorn, of course, was impervious to the weather as he seemed to be to everything
else. He was a natural part of both ship and sea.

"Beorn," I said one day as we sat in the cockpit enjoying
a clear blue afternoon, "what do you do on the trips you
take? Where do you go?"

"I go many places and do many things. A man sees me
and my boat, and he talks to me and says, 'Beorn Wiglafson,

if you will do this thing for me I will pay you money.' I listen to him and if the money is enough and if I wish to do the thing he asks I say, 'Okay, I will do it for you.' And then I do the thing he has asked."

"What sort of things?" I didn't see how one man in so small a boat could actually make a living.

"Oh, many things," he replied in his huge voice. "One winter I sailed for many weeks between islands north of Venezuela carrying guns—rifles and bazookas—from one to the other. Later I carried men to the same island. For this I received many dollars from a man in Puerto Rico. That same year another man asked me to go to that same island again and take away a man who wished to leave there. The man was very frightened when I went and found him at the cove where we were to meet. He looked behind him along the road which led there, but paid me extra money to take aboard boxes and suitcases which he had brought in his car. He did not wish to leave the island without the boxes and suitcases.

"Another time, I am in Denmark at a village I know. A man brings another man and asks if I will take him to England. I know many coves and beaches in England, so I say Yes and take the man with me. At sea I go below and find that the man is dead. There is blood here," Beorn touched himself low on the chest. "I open his clothes and find a wound made by a bullet. In his pocket I find papers and some money but I find no name for the man."

"What did you do?"

He raised a hand negligently, "I decide that since he is dead it will do no good to put him ashore, so I put him overboard. Then I put the money in my pocket. It was not much, and he did not need it."

What an amoral old pirate he was. Still, I was fascinated. "Go on. Tell me more."

Pleased by so receptive an audience, he did go on, and I

heard tales of intrigue mixed with honest trade which took place all over the world. I couldn't believe that one man could have done so much in a single lifetime, yet at the same time there was always the odd ring of truth in his speech.

"Look there, Luther," he said, after he'd been talking for an hour or so. His right forefinger pointed to the cabin behind me. I turned and looked and finally saw a roughness in the paint. Looking closer I could see where a row of holes the size of my finger had been filled and painted over. Seated in the cockpit, the line of holes was about six inches above the top of my head.

"Those are bullet holes!"

"Ya!" His laughter bellowed across the water. "Those come from a machine gun. One night I land in Mexico with some rifles and four men who are to take them inland. I anchor offshore and the men take my dinghy and the rifles and go to shore. But then there is trouble. Policemen, I think, are waiting behind the trees, and when the four men land, one of them is shot and the others are taken. When I see this happen I cut the anchor and turn on the motor and go out of that cove. Policemen shoot after me from the beach, but I am ducking low in the cockpit and the bullets hit there on the cabin. I think maybe I will get my rifle and shoot back, but then I say, 'No, Beorn Wiglafson, is not right for you to shoot,' so I do not. Later I hunt for long time to get the rest of my money, but I did not ever get it all. A funny story, yes?"

"Ho, ho," I said, "very funny."

"Oh, do not look so glum, my young friend. A seafarer does not do such things often. There has been little shooting in my life. I am a trader and a man of peace. I carry gems and guns sometimes, but more often I have skins aboard, or salt, or copra, or people who wish to go to some place where no boats will take them. I trade or buy and sell. I take ivory from Africa and trade it for oils, or oils and trade it for ivory. It is an honorable way to live, I think, and is not without profit."

"Don't you ever wonder what people do with those guns you smuggle?"

He looked at the sails and hauled in the mainsheet a bit, "With such guns men are killed, but what is that to me? If men wish to kill men of their own country, it does not matter. I will carry medicine as soon as guns. It is not the concern of a trader what is done with the goods he carries once they pass from him.

"And when I buy," he added, "it does not matter to me whence the goods came or who might once have possessed them. When they are mine I do with them as I will."

"Do you ever take without paying?" I asked a bit tightly, thinking of my tenuous grip on the *Gate of Horn*.

"Oh, I have sometimes given less than was asked, but I have not taken without paying a fair price." He looked at me from under hairy brows, and his eyes held a curious half-humorous light.

"Where did you get that bag of gold coin that you had in Boston?" I asked hurriedly, changing the subject.

"That was old coin, Luther, and came from an ancient place. . . ." He frowned then, but his eyes still glittered, and I shivered suddenly.

"Forget it," I said, pulling my collar up around my neck. "Tell me a story that happened in some warm place. This air is cold."

He puffed a cloud of smoke and looked at me with his fathomless eyes. "One time," he said, after a moment, "I meet some men who wish to go up a river—the Amazon— in Brazil. They look for the city of old peoples, they say. We go into the land for a long, long time, for the river is wide and deep. . . ."

His voice was old and grand, like the sea itself.

In the latter days of May we began to see sea birds in the air and then an occasional ship on the horizon. We were beginning to work our way back into the shipping lanes as we came in toward the English Channel. Then one day when the sky was clear and the wind steady from the south I climbed the mainmast with a pair of glasses and stayed there for a time looking northeast toward a bank of clouds that lay there. After a while I thought I saw a faint line close to the water, and looked more closely. I felt a wild joy go through me, and looked down at Beorn in the cockpit below.

"Land ho!" I shouted, pointing. It was the first land I'd seen since leaving Boston, and I was amazed at how pleased the sight of it made me.

Below, Beorn grinned and waved, "The Scilly Isles!" he boomed up at me.

I stayed on the mast all that afternoon, watching the islands come closer and then pass behind us to port. Then I scrambled down and got out my charts. Beorn looked over my shoulder and put his big finger on the islands, "Here is the place," he rumbled in my ear, "and now we go here and then on here." His finger slid east and north through the channel toward the North Sea. We grinned at each other; our destination, though still hundreds of miles ahead, seemed suddenly very near.

We began to see many ships and boats as we worked eastward past the Channel Islands, Cherbourg, and Hastings. Off Dover we even got fresh fish from a trawler. She ranged alongside us, asked of our voyage, and her crewmen tossed three long silvery fish across the water between us and into the cockpit. The fish were freshly caught and flopped on the floorboards. Beorn picked one up in each hand and bellowed our thanks as the trawler bore away toward England.

We ate the fish that evening and sailed on through shifting winds, passing finally into the North Sea. The water was cold and storm clouds buffeted us with wind and snowy rain as we beat northeast toward the Skagerrak. Finally the air cleared, however, and I began to feel excitement build up in me when we saw the Danish coast. Between Norway and Denmark we worked eastward and, at last, rounded Skagen, got in front of the north wind, and drove full sailed south down the Kattegat.

It was a hundred and fifty miles to Copenhagen. The voyage was almost over. To port we could distantly see the coast of Sweden, where Beowulf perhaps had ruled his people a thousand years before. I tried to imagine what it must have been like then, when life was short and hard, and the Geats and Danes raided down the coasts of Europe and fought among themselves. Closing my eyes I could see ring-prowed boats with long oars sliding across the cold water, filled with adventurers or coastal ravagers. In my mind, the men were of Beorn's kind: large, powerful, ancient. They bore shields and carried heavy, trusted swords and axes, and their eyes were stolid and watchful and touched with superstition. And on the shore, garbed in battle-dented armor, other men waited for the raiders, watching them come, knowing that some would die on both sides and that only their strength and courage lay between their homeland and the raiders.

I opened my eyes and found the *Gate of Horn* passing islands off to port. An hour later we left the island of Laesø behind us to starboard. "Tomorrow we will be there," smiled Beorn, as he watched me staring at the land through my glasses. "Tomorrow we will be in København."

The next morning brought us down through the straits between Helsingor and Halsingborg, past the island of St. Ibb, and into the Sound.

Four hours later we brought the *Gate of Horn* up into the wind and dropped sail. Beorn got the motor started and we went on in under power, Beorn at the helm while I lashed and stowed sails. The harbor was crowded and busy, and the sounds of ships and commerce rolled across the water. We found an anchorage and put the dinghy over. Beorn got in and rowed ashore while I busied myself tidying up the boat.

Half an hour later, a launch came out from the port authority buildings towing our dinghy. A uniformed man who spoke very good English checked our papers, made a cursory yet thorough inspection of the boat, and bade us welcome to Denmark. When he had gone in the launch, we hauled anchor and took the *Gate of Horn* across harbor.

"I see a man when I go ashore," explained Beorn. "He has dock there"—he pointed ahead—"we will tie up there."

It was an old dock, but solid and well made. Beorn laid the boat lightly alongside, and we made fast. The fenders were hung, and we were there. Beorn cut the engine, locked the hatches, and stepped up to join me on the dock.

"Come," he boomed, flashing his great yellow teeth, "I buy you a drink, yes?"

"Yes, indeed," I said, and we walked away from the boat into the city. It was June seventh. We had three days before Dottie and the professor would be flying in, and at least one of them could well be spent in drinking.

Beorn knew the city and was known by it. Everywhere we went, as we traveled from bar to bar along the waterfront, men would come to our table and greet Beorn. They were a motley crew of every age and nation, and they spoke a half-dozen languages all of which Beorn seemed to know. When Beorn introduced me and told them I was sailing with him, they greeted me with an odd mixture of curiosity and respect.

"He speaks only English," Beorn would then explain, and our visitors, too, would then speak only English.

"You have had a good trip, Beorn?" they would ask, lifting glasses to our health.

"Ya, a fair voyage," Beorn would reply, sometimes looking across the table at me with impenetrable eyes as he spoke. "The money from the trading is in my banks."

"You were a long time at sea. Did you sail east after your cousin?"

"No. I go to the Americas this time; to Panama, to the Islands, to Texas and then"—his eyes would turn from me —"to Boston in the north."

"It is good to have you back, Beorn."

When they returned to their tables, I more than once saw them lean toward other drinking companions and speak. The companions would lift their eyes and look across at us as the conversation continued. Soon Beorn would drain his glass. "Is time to go on, ya?" he would say, and he would get up and lead the way out of the bar, down the street, and into another bar where the cycle of greeting, drinking, conversation, and curious looks would continue.

By the time we got back to the boat I had been introduced to half the wharf dwellers in town, it seemed, and was in sad shape. I think Beorn dumped me in my bunk, because I don't remember getting there myself. My shoes were still on when I woke up late the next morning with a monstrous head and sick belly. I could hear Beorn on deck. He was probably checking lines and fittings, I thought, and suffering no ill effects whatsoever from the previous night's drinking.

I lay there thinking dully of the tales he'd told me of his life and wondered how much he hadn't told. Men seemed to know him wherever he came ashore, and they held him in almost ominous respect. There was Farrow in Boston and these men in Copenhagen, and God knew how many others in ports I'd never seen. In his stories he'd always seem to mention "a man I know" or "a man who find me and ask" such and such. He was a sea rover of the old school, willing to do almost anything if the price was right. Although he'd never come right out and admitted it, I suspected that he was a bit of a pirate on the side. His private code of ethics would allow for that, I thought.

My head was aching steadily and I smelled of drink, salt, and accumulated grime. I thought back on the poker game and was grateful that I'd drunk so little during that time. I would never know how much Beorn must have drunk before the game started, but he had drunk steadily from his black bottle for three days before it ended, and that, I knew, was the only reason he'd ever allowed himself to lose his boat. It would take an unimaginable amount of liquor to affect him that much; last night's binge hadn't troubled him a whit, and he'd had twice what I'd drunk.

Now that he was sober and we were an ocean away from Boston, I realized how tenuous my grip on the boat really was. My only real weapon was the strength of his word that he would work for me during the summer. I had only his sense of honor on my side; my threats of courts and prison were no good at all any more.

And then I realized that they'd really been no good from the time we left Boston harbor. Anytime at all, Beorn could have tossed me overboard and left no one the wiser. I shivered at the thought. The old bastard knew it too! He was no fool.

But then, he *hadn't* thrown me overboard. That was the point. He could have, but didn't. That meant he really was going through with his bargain. I was in no condition to wonder why; rather I simply relaxed and thanked God. For a while I listened to Beorn move around the decks. Then I went to sleep.

In midafternoon, still nursing a terrible hangover, I came on deck with the list of supplies the professor had given me before we left Boston. He and Dot would be coming in two days, and we would be off shortly after that on our way to the Swedish coast. Beorn was seated on the foredeck mending sail with neat, precise stitches. I held up the list and told him what it was. He took it.

"Sit down, Luther. I will go after these goods. It is better, I think, that you rest and bathe, ya? You wait here and gather some clean clothing for yourself. I will send a man to wash our unclean clothing and bedding. He will also tell you how to find a bath."

He smiled and went off into the city. By the time the man came for the clothes, I had every hatch and port open, and most of the bedding and clothing topside airing in the sun. The man took the clothes and blankets, told me in broken English how to find the baths, and went off.

On the way to the baths, I stopped at a pharmacy, told the druggist my problem, and received a remedy which tasted vile but did the job.

The baths were a new experience. The heat and cold cleared out my pores, did away with the remnants of my hangover, and even led me to shave off my now flourishing beard. The girls in the baths surprised me, but I didn't seem to surprise them, so I relaxed and enjoyed it. It is the only way to take a bath, really.

It was late when I got back to the boat, but I felt marvelously fresh and had the boat in pretty good order by the time Beorn came down to the dock with a man driving an old Ford pickup loaded with food and gear. We stowed everything on board and restowed everything we'd taken out that day. That night while Beorn went into the city I stayed on board and got some sleep. The next day, the two of us worked steadily getting everything in order, taking on fuel and water, and preparing for the coming trip up the coast. The *Gate of Horn* was well packed when we finished.

"Is there more to get?" I asked Beorn. We didn't have room for much more. As it was, the boat was going to be crowded with four of us on board.

"No more," said Beorn. "When we leave we take some fresh fruit, maybe; everything else is here."

"Good."

"Ya," Beorn looked at the sun in the west. "Come, we go drink with friends, yes?"

It was tempting, but the professor would be coming in the next day, so I declined.

"You go, Beorn, and lift a few for me. I'll stay here."

He shrugged and smiled, "Rest well then, Luther."

After he'd gone, I enjoyed the last scotch I'd be having for quite a while and went to bed reasonably sober.

Beorn and I were in the passenger terminal when Dot and the professor came through customs. Dot saw us and came to us with a flush of excitement. She clutched our arms and unexpectedly gave each of us an embrace and kiss. Mine was even warm. I was astounded.

"We're here. I really can't believe it! Oh, you both look so well." She tossed her glances between us, "Did you have a good trip? How long have you been in?" I was smiling and dazed; she sounded almost like a normal human being. Finally the professor got to us, shook hands, and broke up her monologue.

"I'm delighted to see you, gentlemen. I trust everything has gone satisfactorily?"

"Ya," said Beorn, shifting his gaze from Dot to her uncle. "We have been in for three days and have the *Gate of Horn* ready with everything you wished."

"Wonderful." Uncle Cyril turned to his niece, "My dear, we'll spend tonight at the hotel. I see no need of delaying our departure longer than that, do you? Tomorrow, then, we'll go." He looked at Beorn and me, "Does that sound satisfactory, gentlemen?"

We nodded.

"I'll have our luggage taken to the hotel, then," said the professor.

"Come and have dinner with us, please," said Dot. "I want to hear all about the trip you've had."

"Yes, do join us," said the professor. "Dot can ask her questions during dinner and then afterward I may have something of interest to show you."

Something of interest?

"We'll be there," I said.

CHAPTER 8

Dot got her history of the trip between bites of the best supper I'd had in months, and afterward we all went up to the professor's room where we could talk in private. Ashman got his briefcase and pulled out a roll of paper.

"This is what I want to show you," he said, and unrolled it.

It was a map of sorts, showing what seemed to be an island off the coast of a larger land mass. Around and upon the drawing of the island were blocks and lines of a writing I could not decipher. The writing was in script, and was worn away in spots.

"This is a copy of the original chart that was found in the manuscripts now at Weststock. I made this copy myself, and I have, in addition, two other photostats of the original in my briefcase." He moved a thin finger along the lines of script, "See here. I've reproduced the original as exactly as possible, even to the character of the writing and to the omission of the worn spots."

I looked at the map, curiously stimulated as men always are when confronted by such things, yet highly sceptical. I'd once paid a man thirty-five dollars for a better map than this, and soon found out that he'd sold a dozen others just like it to other suckers before leaving town.

"What is this?" I asked, as Beorn and I leaned forward for a better look.

"It is a map of an island I believe to be off the western coast of Sweden," said the professor. "And I believe that it is the key to the discovery of Beowulf's tomb. Look here!" His finger touched the line marking the coastline. "See these two headlands? And here, see these markings? I believe they indicate a causeway of sorts linking the island to the mainland. Have you read a fragment called the *Battle of Malden*? This causeway seems to me to be much like the one mentioned in *Malden:* a sand bar, probably, possibly reinforced by stone and mortar to some extent, but a causeway, nevertheless, by which, at low tide at least, persons on the island could pass across to the mainland!"

His voice, touched by excitement, flowed on, and his long scholar's hands moved across the map. "See here. On the island there is an indication of a town, or of the ruins of one. And this script here, with the pointing arrow, tells that it is a place where 'an ancient people dwelled.'"

"What language is it?" I interrupted.

"Ah." The professor's eyes flashed up at me and Beorn, who sat stolidly, his face expressionless, looking at the map, "I forgot that you don't read it. It's primarily Middle English. Surely you've read the *Canterbury Tales?* This is the same language, but in script rather than print. But note this" —he touched segments of script—"these words and phrases are Old English! When I noted these phrases, I was sure that the map was possibly more important than it first seemed; apparently it is a copy of an even older map. The chart found in the Weststock collection—the one which I've copied for us here—was probably made in the fourteenth century. Everyone who's studied the chart agrees with that, and as you know, they agree with me about very little else." His voice was touched fleetingly with bitterness, "It is my contention that the person who made the Weststock map

wrote in Middle English, and that he copied a map originally
written in Old English. Those words or phrases with which
he was unfamiliar he left in their original form; the rest he
translated into his own language. The original map has probably long since been lost, and only the copied map survived. It was only luck that we found it."

"What is the importance of this island?" rumbled Beorn,
an odd note of curiosity in his voice. "I have read the book
of Beowulf which you gave me and found no talk there of
islands."

"A very good question," said the professor, sitting back,
"and one which has prevented many of my colleagues from
sharing my enthusiasm for the theory I hope to prove on the
coming voyage. I believe, gentlemen, that this island was
once the location of a major town in Geatland, and that
upon one of those headlands on the shore behind it we will
find the burial place of the Geatish chieftain who was called,
by the poet at least, 'Beowulf.' I also believe that upon the
other headland we shall find a burial crypt from an even
older civilization. You say you have finished the book I gave
you, Beorn?"

"Ya," said Beorn, his ageless eyes bright.

"Then you have read of Beowulf's battle with the dragon,
and of his burial in fire and of the tower his men built
over him. Now I will tell you more."

He dug out a cigarette and lit it. Dot got up and fixed
scotch for the three of them while the professor leaned forward and began to lecture as if he were in front of a class
at Weststock. The first portion of his remarks dealt with
the history of the manuscript and covered the same ground
that Dot had covered with me two months before in her
apartment, but by the time he'd finished his first cigarette
and started another, he was inching into new territory.

". . . The *Beowulf* poem is almost the only document
extant which gives the modern historian or scholar any in-

formation at all about Scandinavia during the years of the early Dark Ages. Save what the poem tells us, we have almost no knowledge of the years between 200 and 400 A.D. in Scandinavia. That period of time is simply closed off to us. Writing was almost nonexistent and whatever records might have been kept have been lost long since. Rome was withdrawing her legions from the north, and the barbarians were sweeping over Europe and destroying or fundamentally changing whatever civilization existed there. All knowledge of letters was swept away, and a very real darkness of ignorance and superstition came down across northern Europe. Out of this, we have only a single long song and a few fragments to tell us of the life and activities of the people who dwelt in that land during that time.

"But a poem is not history, or so historians often believe. Certainly it is not history in the sense that we usually use the term. Rather it is a mixture of facts and fictions told by a poet whose greatest interest is, in the case of an epic such as *Beowulf* at least, in the grandeur of his themes rather than in the accuracy of his events. However, of late, historians have had to look again at some of the old poems they might once have dismissed as purely imaginative writings.

"From Homer's accounts of the battle of Troy, scholars have actually found the city itself, and in their excavations they have discovered that Homer's measures and distances are remarkably accurate. More recently, another man has taken a sailing vessel and, by following the routes described in the *Odyssey,* has established a strong case for the authenticity of that poem's detail and description of lands and occurrences encountered by Odysseus.

"From the Bible and the scrolls discovered in the caves above the Dead Sea, other scholars have found places once thought to be mythical or imagined. Even now, another group of scholars—classicists among them—are combining

Plato's commentary with modern research methods and are excavating on a Greek island with every confidence that they've found the ruins of the civilization Plato called 'Atlantis.'

❧ "Is *Beowulf* then to be thought of differently? Is it, after all, only a song made up from whole cloth and sung only for the pleasure of its listeners? I think not. There is, after all, other data—the *Historia Francorum* and the rest—which proves that some of the poem, at least, deals with historical fact. I am convinced that the poem is essentially accurate in its history!"

The professor's eyes glowed behind his glasses. Beorn was listening with intense, expressionless interest. As it had been on the *Gate of Horn* when he read the book, his mind seemed to be reaching back into its memories and linking some ancient recollection to what he was learning now.

"Within the poem itself," the professor went on, "there are certain phrases and words which are not completely agreed upon as to their meaning. Different scholars translate them in different manners and arrive, naturally enough, at different interpretations of some lines of the poem. The translation I gave you, Beorn, is that of a fine poet who has captured all of the vigor and tragedy of the song and put it into modern English. It is a fine translation, but makes no attempt to be literal.

"I made my first translation years ago, when I was completing my thesis, and even at that time I was sure that certain passages of the poem deserved translation other than that more popularly agreed upon. One section specifically is relevant to us here: The word *ealond,* which appears in the section of the poem dealt with in lines 2333 to 2335. In Old English, the poem reads, '*Haefde ligdraca leoda laesten, eoland utan, eorðweall ðone gledun forgrunden.*'" The words rolled out of his mouth in a tumbling stream, and he went on without pausing, "Now many translators interpret those lines as meaning something like, 'The fire dragon had with flames destroyed the fortress of the people and the shore.' Your translation, for example, Beorn, says:

> 'But the hall was gone, the dragon's molten
> Breath had licked across it, burned it
> To ashes, near the shore it had guarded'

"However, such translations err in one important respect, I firmly believe: The word *ealond*, which editors translate by 'shore' or 'seaboard,' is, actually, a rather common word which always means 'island.' A correct interpretation of the passage would read, 'The fire dragon had with flames destroyed the fortress of the people, the island all around, and its earthen rampart.'" The professor looked at us, his voice touched with excitement.

"Do you understand the significance of that single difference in translation? It suggests that at least a major Geatish town or fortress was located on an island, and not, as is generally supposed, on the mainland of what is now Sweden.

"And there is more: In the description of the dragon's barrow where the treasure was hidden, and of Beowulf's battle and later burial, we are told, in the *Cotton Vitellius* if not in every translation, that the battle took place on a cliff called *Earna-noes*, Eagle's Ness, and that after the fight Beowulf lay on flat ground, *wong-stede*, while the dragon fell near the treasure hoard, *hord-oerne nēah*, opposite, *wiðer-roehtes*, the spot where Beowulf lay.

"The wood where the group of cowardly Geats waited was on the summit of another headland, and afterward they went *under Earna-noes* and found Beowulf *on sande*.

"The dragon's barrow crowned the pinnacle of the cliff where the battle was fought, and afterward the dragon's body was rolled off the headland into the sea. Beowulf's body was burned on a neighboring headland called the Whale's Ness, and his tower was placed at the edge of the cliff in a conspicuous position, *oet brinēs nōsan*. Extant barrows and mounds are found in such spots in several countries, and are consistent to those described in the poem!"

The professor's fingers spread across the map before him, "What we have in the poem, gentlemen, is a description of two headlands, and of an island nearby. Upon the island was a fortress of the Geats. Upon one headland was an ancient barrow, filled, the poem tells us, with old treasure guarded by a dragon; upon the other headland was built a burial vault and a tower which could be seen far at sea.

"Here, gentlemen, is a map which fits with remarkable accuracy the description of the scene given us in the poem!"

His face was tense and his voice strained with pride and excitement. Dot, I discovered, was gripping my arm tightly and Beorn was staring at the map, his great gray-black beard brushing the table top.

"If this map is accurate," the professor continued, "we have a good chance to find the tomb, if, indeed, it does exist. The map is really the *raison d'être* for this expedition, for without it, no matter how strong my conviction of the historicity of the hero and his burial, I would simply have no way of knowing where to look or what to look for. There are hundreds of headlands on the coast of Sweden, and, even now, I have no idea how many of them have islands lying offshore. Without a map such as this, no one would know where to begin his search.

"But with this chart, I believe we have a genuine opportunity for success. There are measures of distance in the writing on the chart, and, as you see, a rather carefully drawn map of the island itself and of its landmarks—this cove, for instance, and this hill on the eastward side. And see here; the headlands are split by this oddly shaped inlet. Look at it closely and I'm sure you'll agree that the area is distinctive in appearance, and that by sailing slowly along the coast we have a very good chance of finding it!"

Dot discovered that she was clinging to my arm and detached herself quickly. "What do you think, Lute? Do you think you can find it? Imagine what it would be like!"

"Hmmmm," I muttered, looking thoughtful. My mind was racing backward as I tried to visualize the dozens of named and unnamed islands I'd seen in the Caribbean and, more recently, along the coast of Europe. Islands just aren't that distinctive, I knew. Unless you knew the waters or the island itself, you could land somewhere else entirely. Sweden wasn't my territory; I looked at Beorn, my trusty crew. It was really up to him.

"What do you think, Beorn?"

Beorn stroked his beard and looked at the map. His eyes were deep beneath his brows and were touched by a strange humor.

"Is important that you find this place," he asked finally, encompassing Dot and the professor in a sudden stare.

"Yes, Beorn," said Uncle Cyril. "I believe it could be one of the most significant scholarly discoveries of our age."

"Is gold and treasure, eh?"

"That's not the important thing, Beorn," said Dot with a smile. "The importance is in finding the place where Beowulf lived and died. For a thousand years men have heard about him, but we are the first to have a chance to prove to the world that he was a real king and that the poem is true!"

Uncle Cyril was genuinely shocked by Beorn's reference to treasure. "Good heavens," he exclaimed, "we aren't gold seekers! Even if we do happen to find some portion of the treasure, it could never be ours; it would go to a museum or to a university for display and study!"

"My pardon, professor," rumbled Beorn, with a slight inclination of his head. Uncle Cyril seemed pacified by this slight gesture. "I know this coast," continued Beorn. "Perhaps the island you seek is there, yes?"

"Yes," exclaimed Uncle Cyril. Then looking at me, "We can sail tomorrow, then?"

I was thinking of Beorn. "What?" I asked. Then, "Tomorrow it is, sir. All the supplies are on board."

"Marvelous."

Then for the rest of the evening I irritably sipped black coffee and watched the other three grow comradely on scotch and soda as they talked about the expedition.

We cleared harbor the next day, passing beyond the little mermaid that sits on her stone charming everyone who sees her, and beat against headwinds toward the Swedish coast. In the middle of the Sound, we crossed to a starboard tack and pounded up toward the straits off Helsingor where, according to the Bard, Hamlet, Prince of Denmark, once disposed of his family and himself. The wind was touched with summer, but the *Gate of Horn* was slow so we had a lot of time to answer Dot's questions about the boat. She'd never sailed before and was interested in everything. She kept Beorn and me busy telling her what did what, and why, getting her to call lines lines instead of ropes, explaining theory and whatnot. Unlike Caribbean cruise girls who'd asked the same questions, she remembered what she was told and kept her eyes open, so that by the time we cleared the straits and once more came around to the northeast she'd learned to keep out of the way and actually was some help. In the galley she produced coffee and fixed a midafternoon meal that was far superior to what Beorn and I were used to fixing for ourselves. She had a feel for sail and adapted quickly. Beorn watched her with admiring eyes.

We'd given Dot the bunk space forward of the main cabin, and the rest of us were sharing the two bunks in the cabin; with a man on watch most of the time, no more than two of us would be sleeping at any one time, so the professor and I tended to share my bunk and leave Beorn's to him. The morning before we cleared port, I'd removed all that remained of my private liquor supply from under the bunk and hidden it away in the forward sail locker. When he'd stowed his gear, the professor had discovered the place where I'd been keeping my stuff and promptly put his own supply in. It was a good spot for booze all right, and the old buzzard had noticed it immediately.

The wind dropped a bit toward evening and the *Gate of Horn* straightened up and plowed smoothly toward the Swedish coast. Dot talked Beorn into letting her take the helm and laughed at the pull of the tiller in her hands. Beorn sat beside her like a great bear, talking to her and pointing with his huge hands. He told her she must watch the sails, look to the lee and windward, keep an eye on the compass, and watch where she was going. She listened carefully and tried to do everything at once.

It seemed like a good time for me to get down to work so I got Uncle Cyril down into the cabin with me, and got a photostat of his chart.

"I'll need this," I said, laying it on the table which swung between the bunks. "And I need some help from you. I want you to write down a translation of all the writing on this chart. Put the translation beside the original so I'll know exactly what says what."

"Very good," he replied, and began to write. I watched him slash out line after line of sloppy scholastic script and was once again positive that, next to physicians, college professors have the worst handwriting in the world. Still, I could, with effort, read what he wrote, and when he was finished I pulled the chart in front of me and began to study it. There wasn't much that would help me find the island, I discovered very quickly. Still, I had to learn it by heart if we wanted to find the place. Any information was better than none.

CHAPTER 9

"I've not tried to give anything but a translation that is correct in meaning," Uncle Cyril said a bit apologetically. "The meter hasn't been reproduced, and I've not tried to be exact in imagery."

"That's fine," I said, "I need to know facts, if there are any here. The poetry can wait for a while."

"I understand, captain."

Captain? Beorn should have a translated copy, too, I thought.

A wormlike sea serpent adorned one portion of the sea. On the bottom of the chart were the words, "From here came *Yrmenlaf* of Danes." That helped, if the bottom of the chart was south as I took it to be. Since the line marking the mainland behind the island was at the top of the chart, the island then was lying off a coastline that ran roughly from south to north or southeast to northwest. The west coast of Sweden was, then, the place to look. The coastline was irregular and could easily contain a portion of shore matching that on the chart.

On the drawing of the mainland was the word "Geatland." So far, so good. As far as I'd been able to tell from my reading and from the professor's talks, it was generally supposed that the Geats had lived in southern Sweden, although no one seemed to know exactly where. It was logical to assume that Beowulf's people, being seafarers, had settled on the shore as well as inland.

On the drawing of the island were several phrases which described the island in a roundabout way. The island itself was roughly the shape of the continent of Africa or like a lopsided pear with its heavy end nearest the mainland. On its outermost point was the word "tower." I put my finger on it.

"Undoubtedly a watchtower from which an observer could look out to sea," said the professor, leaning over the map. "I presume, therefore, that that portion of the island is high land. A watchman could see some distance and would have ample opportunity to warn of approaching ships."

"And the people he'd warn would be those in this town."

"Correct."

The town was marked by a few sketchy lines on the side of the island nearest the mainland. Beside it were the lines, "Here dwelled Higelac, loved by his thanes, perilous to his enemies. Before him, an ancient people built high walls here before they perished." Higelac had been king of the Geats long before Beowulf took the crown.

The chart indicated the link between the island and the mainland that the professor had mentioned before. Beside the markings indicating the link was a longish piece of writing: "This bridge was built by God who built the seas, and was built again by ancient people who once dwelled here. On this bridge Higelac's thanes could laugh at foes or slay them if they came too near their spears. . . ." There was a gap in the lines where words had been worn away, then the lines continued briefly, ". . . Here Weohstan and his warriors fought twenty waves of Swedish soldiers, mighty men with spearshields who struck with endless blows. . . ."

"Who was Weohstan?" I asked.

"We can't be sure, but the name is mentioned in *Beowulf* as being that of a Geatish warrior, the father, in fact, of Wiglaf, the young man who went to aid Beowulf against the dragon. It may not be the same man at all; the name was not uncommon.

"After the death of Beowulf, the Swedes finally overran the Geats and destroyed them. This island might have been the site of a battle in the final war, and Weohstan may have been the Geatish commander during that action."

"Horatio at the bridge."

"Not a bridge at all, really. The phrase 'built by God who built the seas' suggests that the original bridge was probably a sand bar which linked the island to the shore at low tide. A similar bridge is mentioned in the *Battle of Malden*, as I believe I told you. In that fragment, which is of a later date than *Beowulf* but which deals with similar people and conditions, the British leader Byrhtnoth is called upon to repel a group of Danish raiders who have landed on a small island linked by a 'bridge' to the shore. Byrhtnoth and his men easily hold against them until Byrhtnoth, in a fit of pride, pulls his men back and allows the raiders to cross the bridge and fight on shore. Byrhtnoth is killed and his men are defeated.

"The bridge in that song is a spit of sand, and this bridge seems much the same. This one, however, apparently was reinforced by human hands. The writing here suggests that an unnamed ancient people who apparently lived on the island before the Geats built it up in some way. It may be that a causeway was built on the foundation of the sand spit."

Something was trying to form in my brain, but before I could puzzle it out, the professor identified it for me:

"You'll remember, also, that in *Beowulf* we're told that the dragon is guarding a treasure placed in the barrow by 'the last of a noble race.' The *Beowulf* poet definitely identifies him as being of stock other than Geatish, Swedish, Danish, or any other known people. Rather, he was a last surviving member of a once rich and powerful people whose name was unknown to the poet . . ."

His voice went on, but I was remembering the poem and did not hear him.

> That tower
> Was heaped high with hidden treasure, stored there
> Years before by the last survivor
> Of a noble race, ancient riches
> Left in the darkness as the end of a dynasty
> Came. Death had taken them, one
> By one, and the warrior who watched over all
> That remained mourned their fate, expecting,
> Soon, the same for himself, knowing
> The gold and jewels he had guarded so long
> Could not bring him pleasure much longer. He brought
> The precious cups, the armor, and the ancient
> Swords, to a stone tower built
> Near the sea, below a cliff, a sealed
> Fortress with no windows, no doors, waves
> In front of it, rocks behind. Then he spoke:
> "Take these treasures, earth, now that no one
> Living can enjoy them. They were yours, in the beginning;
> Allow them to return.

> .   .   .   .   .

> The harp's
> Bright song, the hawk crossing through the hall
> On its swift wings, the stallion tramping
> In the courtyard—all gone, creatures of every
> Kind, and their masters, hurled to the grave!"
> And so he spoke, sadly, of those
> Long dead, and lived from day to day,
> Joyless, until, at last, death touched
> His heart and took him too. And a stalker
> In the night, a flaming dragon, found
> The treasure unguarded. . . .

The professor was blinking his scholar's eyes at me and talking, "It is my contention that the ancient people mentioned on this chart were probably the same group mentioned in *Beowulf*. It all fits together, does it not? Imagine this with me: Sometime in the distant past, in the very early Dark Ages or possibly before—before the Geatish civilization at any rate—a group of people founded a culture of some sort on the coast of Sweden. They built a fortress city on the island shown on this chart where they lived amid some accumulation of wealth. Later, for a reason we can only guess at—disease, perhaps, or wars—they perished or left the country. The last survivor of this race gathered together the remaining treasures of his people and hid them in a barrow high on a headland above the island. His motives, I think, would have been first to secure the treasure for the future return of his people, and second to put it in a place which the enemies of his people would be unlikely to find. The natural place for such enemies or treasure seekers to look would be on the island itself, since it was there that the city existed. Few, if any would think of looking high up on a coastal headland.

"Later, the Geats began developing their culture along the coast, and being intelligent people living in perilous times, saw the advantages of the island and built their own city there. Finally, when the dragon—if there was one literally—took up living in the barrow and was discovered and robbed by a slave—possibly a slave seeking escape by climbing a steep headland to elude his master. The city below was ravished and Beowulf, the old king, went out and fought his last battle on the headland, below the dragon's barrow. The treasure that had brought about the destruction of their city and the death of their king was then carried by the Geats to the nearby headland where the king was given a Viking funeral of fire, and was thrown into the burial tower with the bones of Beowulf. The Geats would want no part of the fortune, for it had brought nothing but tragedy to them, and they would, in addition, wish to keep it from the Swedes who were even then preparing to come down upon them and destroy them."

He paused and looked at me. "That is my theory," he concluded.

There was a weird logic to it if you granted his premises, and the chart seemed to back him up. If it were real. I had some more questions. "But who were these ancient people who were here before the Geats? Do you have any idea?"

An owlish look came into his eyes, "I can't be sure, of course; and that is one of the reasons this trip is so important. If I can discover the island, I can perhaps find evidence of who the people were. That in itself would be a major scholastic and historic find. Whoever they were, they must surely have left some tools or wares that would allow us to identify them. And whoever they were, I'm sure they must have come by ship; there is no other logical way for them to have arrived. If they had come overland, they would have had to pass far to the north, across what is now Lapland in northern Sweden and Finland, and then come far south again to this area. A few adventurers from Asia might well have done just that, of course, but this civilization was not that of a group of adventurers. It was apparently much more complex and developed than that. The *Beowulf* poet lists considerable treasure found in the dragon's barrow. No group of adventurers would or could accumulate such treasure on so barren a coast as this. Rather, it was the wealth of a major colony sufficiently advanced to build an island city and a causeway linking it to the mainland.

"I'm sure, therefore, that this pre-Geatish people must have come by sea from the south—from France or Germany perhaps, or possibly from even farther south. The Romans were spreading to all parts of the world at that time, remember, and other Mediterranean and Eastern nations were trading widely throughout the known world. Not a few nations were seeking a northeast passage to the Orient and were sending their ships out to found colonies for trade and exploration. It is from some such nation, I think, that the island city was founded."

The old bastard was making my spine tingle, which annoyed me. "What about the dragon? Do you have an explanation about that too?"

He allowed himself a thin smile, "I am not a superstitious man, Mr. Martingale. I do not believe in ghosts or trolls or monsters. However, it is well known that people who tend to believe the world to be a certain way also tend to see things in that world which support their beliefs. A person who believes that dragons are real, for example, might well tend to see them where sceptics would not. The fire-spitting dragon is a widely used symbol throughout the world, as I'm sure you know. The oriental dragon is well known to us all, as is the European dragon of St. George or Uther Pendragon, the father of Arthur of Britain. Mariners setting out on unknown seas confidently expected to encounter dragons of the deep, and even today the 'sea monster' is not an unknown commodity. The Loch Ness Monster not only receives annual press coverage but has been photographed and detected on underwater sonic devices. . . ."

"All right," I interrupted, "I get the picture."

"Perhaps you do," said the professor testily, "but let me give you just a few historical examples in addition to those we've already mentioned. They may give you a better sense of the temper of our forefathers' realm of belief.

"There is a great deal of what some writers have called 'dragon lore' in the history of Europe. In the Cotton Gnomic verses, for example, we are told that the proper place for a dragon is in a grave mound, brooding over treasure. Does that ring a familiar bell in you, young man? If so, you might also be interested to know that in the large chambered

Tumulous of Maeshow in Orkney which, according to some runic inscriptions on its walls, seems once to have contained much treasure; there is actually a picture of a dragon drawn with a good deal of primitive skill. Very Beowulfish, I'm sure you'll agree."

I nodded, and he continued, "*The Anglo Saxon Chronicle* informs us that, in the year 793, the people of Northumbria beheld a dragon in the air and were distressed lest their crops suffer from its presence. The modern viewer would not, I dare say, share their interpretation; he might, instead, call the object a flying saucer, don't you think?" Heavy sarcasm was not his strong suit, but he went on anyway, "Belief in the presence of dragons in burial mounds continued for many centuries. According to Thomas of Walsingham, a dragon guarding the barrow of Wornelow near Ludlow in 1344 was overcome by the magic of a Saracen physician, and a large store of gold was recovered."

"Stop, stop," I said, grinning in spite of myself and holding up both hands. To my surprise, he did.

"Very interesting," I said finally.

"Yes. The stories are interesting, but the hard fact is this: As far as I know, I am the only person in the academic world who is convinced of the historicity of Beowulf and of the civilization that preceded his. Unless I find solid evidence to support my theory, I stand little chance of convincing my colleagues that I am correct, or of getting funds somewhere for a major project of exploration."

"How much do we need to find on this trip?"

He shrugged, "The island and the headlands, of course. If we find those in time, we may have time to look for the barrow and, most importantly, for the tomb itself. We'll need artifacts as well, of course, to show to potential backers." He leaned over the chart, "See here," he pointed to the more eastern headland and to the brief writing beside it. I read 'Whales Ness. Here the king climbed to Heaven on a tower of smoke.'

"No mention of treasure or of dragons here," I pointed out.

"I agree," he said. "But then, if I were fearful of dragons and of Swedes I might not wish to indicate the position of treasure. Be that as it may, this chart corresponds very closely to the facts in the poem. If we can find this place, I believe we will find still more: perhaps evidence of a truth that has lain dead for a thousand years!" Then he leaned forward toward me, "I depend upon you, my boy."

From captain to my boy. Yet, my mind was still caught up in the web of his rhetoric. "Thank you," I said. "If you'll leave me alone now, I'd better get at this map. If we do find that island, I want to know it when I see it."

He went up on deck to join the others, and I put part of my mind to the chart. The other part, however, entertained itself with curious academic fantasy:

Two coeds put their heads together in the hallway and looked after the crisply walking young man.

"That's Professor Martingale!"

"Yes! Isn't he young! Why, I understand that he's the youngest full professor Weststock has ever had."

"He is! He was the leader of the expedition that discovered the tomb of Beowulf, you know, and uncovered that marvelous ruin they had on the cover of *Life*. Why I guess he could have his pick of colleges after that. Harvard and everybody wanted him to teach for *them!*"

"I hear they found a fabulous old treasure!"

"Yes!"

"Oh my! You don't say!"

Oh my. You don't say. You are an ass, Luther. Still, it was some time before I could focus completely on the map.

"The wind is free," I said to Dot.

"And a good thing, too," she agreed, "I hate to think of what it would be costing us if this were a power boat of some kind. Thank goodness for the *Gate of Horn;* she can cruise forever without costing a cent for fuel. You can't imagine how glad I am that you bought a sailboat instead of a cruiser or something."

We were beating slowly north along the coast. Off to starboard the beaches and hills of Sweden lay in a mist which turned them gray and forlorn. Beorn was at the helm and Dot and I were forward, standing on the foredeck and leaning against the mast. The wind was cool from the north, and the water was rolling under us in long blue swells.

"Sail is the only way to go," I said, tucking my arm through hers. She leaned against me a bit and looked aloft. She had taken to the sea and to the boat with amazing rapidity, seeming to feel both in her bones. All good sailors are like that. They sail by instinct and by a kind of misbegotten love that sets them apart from other seafarers and landsmen. I had a bit of it in me, but Dot was a natural, as was Beorn. The two of them, she and Beorn, could already sail as well as Beorn and I, and they struck it off well together. Beorn watched her often; even now I could feel his eyes on our backs. But he never touched her, nor she him. Sticking hard to her statement of engagement, yet unwilling to release the cool intellectual control she kept over herself, she reserved her cheek for my kisses alone.

But her natural bent was elsewhere, and was growing more so as the days on the *Gate of Horn* passed. She warmed to the sea and to sailing and perhaps to more, but not to me. Now, feeling her long, firm body lean against me, I slipped an arm around her waist and flattened my hand across her stomach. She closed her hands over mine and pressed it onto her sweater.

"I'm glad you're a sailor, Lute," she said, and turned

neatly out of my arm with a little laugh. "Wait until fall, dear," she smiled tartly.

"Witch," I said.

"What?"

"Nothing."

She shrugged, "I guess I'll go back and take the tiller for a while. Your crew looks lonely."

I stared at the shore awhile, then turned and looked back at her. She was holding the tiller with both hands, and laughing as the wind whipped her hair.

We inched along the coast for seventeen days, working northward close to shore. At dusk the professor had us drop anchor for fear we might miss our target if we sailed at night. There was little night, actually, for the summer sun was long in the sky and things were fairly light even at midnight. Still, in the dusk we would anchor and Dot and the professor would sleep while Beorn and I stood lazy watches in the cockpit. It was on these watches, when the world was in an odd half-light, that I began to sense the meaning of a Dark Age. I thought it must have been dark literally as well as figuratively, especially in the endless winter nights when day showed itself only briefly and coldly on the southern horizon and then disappeared again into the cold earth or sea. How many battles were fought in darkness, I wondered, and how many men left their homes and simply disappeared into the darkness that never left the land.

It was no surprise that men of those times, unlettered, unable to know anything of the world beyond their senses, except for what old men and bards told of past days and far lands, were so filled with fatalism and superstition. In literal darkness, it is easy to accustom yourself to the fragility of life, to the necessity of bravery, and to the ready belief in monsters. How else could a man of that time feel? Without books to tell him of his history, to keep his mind sure, in the accumulated experience of the men who preceded him and wrote down their experience, he was, in every generation, a First Man in an unknown world.

How savage it must have been, with men on the edge of death all their lives, surrounded not only by the elemental earth itself, but by other strange men bent on their survival at the cost of his. How rare that a tribe could form; how rarer that it could survive. Everything depended on watchmen and warriors.

> High on a wall a Danish watcher
> Patrolling along the cliffs saw
> The travellers crossing to the shore, their shields
> Raised and shining; he came riding down,
> Hrothgar's lieutenant, spurring his horse,
> Needing to know why they'd landed, these men
> In armor. . . .

Men alone, without history. No wonder that the bards sang of heroes, for the people were in need of heroes to prove by their might and valor that men could survive or, failing that, could, in death, triumph against their enemies and, nearly, death itself.

In the dim half-light of the Scandinavian night, I imagined the men in their sewn-skin robes and rare, cherished armor, moving along the shores in search of whatever fortune they might find, or sailing across the waters to lands they only guessed existed. The waters ended, they would imagine, and if they sailed too far, they would fall off the earth; or be swallowed by the monsters that lived in the endless waves and had eaten other ships before theirs.

And how rare and valuable women must have been to such men. No wonder they raided for woman, or that they fought to the death in protecting their own. A woman strong enough to survive and bear sons and daughters was a possession beyond all others, even beyond gold. I thought of Freaw, Welthow, Yrs. . . .

And the weapons. In a land where iron was rare and iron-craft rarer still, how invaluable a good sword or ax must have been to its owner. No wonder that the warriors gave names to their arms, and passed them down to their sons as the most honored of inheritances.

> Healfdane's son gave Beowulf a golden
> Banner, a fitting flag to signal
> His victory, and gave him, as well, a helmet,
> And a coat of mail, and an ancient sword;

Ring-prowed ships, mighty warriors, gold-haired women, ancient weapons—how the poet sang of you.

And it was during one of those long watches, as we bobbed at anchor in some unnamed cove along the coast of that ancient land, that I looked up suddenly from a half dream, and stifled a cry as a Geatish warrior loomed up over me and, huge and bearded against the night sky, reached toward me with a massive warrior's hand.

I struck at the hand and jolted back against the tiller.

"Ah. You sleep, eh? Go below, Luther. I will take watch now."

Beorn!

Below, on the bunk, I shut my eyes and saw him in seal-skins and leggings, a double-bitted war ax in his hand. Beorn the Geat! The vision was sharp in my mind as I went to sleep.

CHAPTER 10

Every headland along that rugged, fiord-broken, undulating coastline had to be investigated, and every island examined. Watchful for shoals and hidden rocks, alert to tides or currents that might put us ashore for good, we closed with the coast again and again, scanning the shore with glasses in hopes of seeing some sign that our search was ended. But always we found nothing. Occasionally I would bring the *Gate of Horn* alongside some fisherman and have Beorn ask him if he knew of an island such as we sought lying off two headlands. Beorn would rumble a query across the water and the fisherman would gesture and reply. Twice we heard of headlands and islands from such fishermen and sought them out only to find that they were not what we were searching for. And half a dozen times we followed deep fiords into the coast in search of rumored but nonexistent places.

The professor was growing impatient as his summer slipped behind him. With my entrance to Weststock assured, I should have been more relaxed, but instead I too became more irritable. The image of Beorn looming over me lingered in my mind and drew me deeper into a vision of the ancient days of Higlac and Herdred, the Geatish kings who had led their people on this very coast a thousand years ago. I began to share something of the professor's obsession with the island, and brooded on the hope of actually stepping onto the very place where the last of the Geatish kings had lived and ruled.

I read the poem again and again, and it came to life in my brain, with giant figures of real men and monsters stalking through mighty halls and across steaming meres. Often I climbed to mast-top and swayed there with binoculars staring at the coastline off to our right. The days turned sharp and clear and the wind held steadily from the northwest.

"Thank God for clear air, at least," I said to the professor one day as we stood on the foredeck. "In fog or rain we could sail past a hundred islands and never see them."

"Yes," he said. "At least we have that in our favor. I only wish we had a hundred more days of weather as good as this. Time grows short."

That night he could not sleep, and instead stayed in the cockpit with Beorn on his watch and then with me on mine. He was restless in the half-light of the Scandinavian night and stared at the shore of the cove we had anchored in.

"We should sail at night, too," he mused.

"I think we might miss the island if we did," I said.

He turned sharply toward me, "We haven't time, Martingale! We've barely touched this coastline. There are hundreds of miles still to search. We must have more time!"

"It will do us no good to sail a thousand miles if we miss the one mile we're looking for."

"I know that. But Beorn and you can bring the boat closer to land during the night so we'll miss nothing. Then if we see anything at all that looks promising we can anchor and investigate during the daylight."

"Too dangerous," I said. "We don't know this coast well enough to hug the shore at night. A rock or a shoal could break us or sink us, or a current could send us aground before we knew what we were about."

"Damn the danger!" His thin hand closed into a fist. "We have to risk it!" He leaned toward me, his glasses forming two tiny mirrors in the light of the night sky. "Unless we sail twenty-four hours a day, we will run out of time before we have a real chance to find it!"

He was right, of course, but I was reluctant to admit it. I had no desire to lose the boat and no real confidence that Beorn would even agree to run the risk. There was nothing besides his questionable sense of honor to keep him with us anyway, and if he thought that I was risking his boat he could very well drop the pretense of being my crewman and simply take over command. If he did decide to do that, there was little I could do about it; I had already lost one fight to him and had no desire to try another one.

"I'll talk to Beorn," I said. "He knows this coast better than I do. If he agrees that we can take the risk, I'll consider it; if he doesn't agree, I'm afraid I can't risk it."

"Who is captain here?" he cried. "You or Beorn? It is your decision, not his!"

"Correct," I lied, "but no captain ignores the opinions of a crewman as good as Beorn. Knowing this coast as he does, I would be a fool to ignore his opinion." I looked severe, "My first duty is to the boat and her passengers, and I won't risk them needlessly."

"Damn!" He pounded his fist on the cabin and stared at the shoreline.

"When Beorn comes on his watch, I'll put it to him," I said.

He stood for a time in silence. "Very well," he said at last. "I certainly cannot sail this vessel myself. I must do as you wish."

"Go below and get some sleep," I said. "I'll speak to Beorn when he comes up."

"I can't sleep tonight. I can't bear the thought of failing because of time!" He turned to me, "Do you realize what this trip means to me? For years I've been trying to get backing for an expedition. When you came to me in April it was like a gift from the gods! I knew even then, of course, that we would be cutting it close to the line with only this boat and a small crew, but I knew I would probably never get another chance even as good as this one."

He was talking more freely than I'd ever heard him, and seemed almost unconscious of the fact that I had ears and heard. I might as well have been a part of the boat or of the sea itself, for he was speaking to himself as much as to me.

"When they found out I was coming over here this summer without backing they all looked sceptical but wished me well. If only I had time! How I dread the thought of returning to face them with nothing!"

He spun around, "Do you know how much a professor—a full professor—makes at Weststock? Less than a good truck driver! I've saved for years for this chance, and I've put every cent I could save or borrow into it. If I fail, I'll be an old man before I can ever come again. I must know, at least, that I am wrong in my theory. I could live with that knowledge, I think, but I would find it unbearable to live with the knowledge that I failed simply because of time, simply because the summer ended too soon. I would never know but that the next headland, the one I did not reach, was the one I sought."

I felt a stirring of sympathy for him. He was being driven by a fear common to the treasure seeker: that circumstances, not fact, would prevent him from reaching his dream. In the west, on the deserts and in the mountains, there are still men who spend their lives futilely seeking a cache or lode that they know must be there just beyond their reach, just over the next rise or beneath the next rimrock. I'd met men like that, and seen in them the touch of fear that was now in the professor: the fear that their faith was right but that fate would turn them back short of their goal.

"We'll find it," I said. "I'll speak to Beorn about night sailing."

He muttered something, perhaps a "thank you," stood silent for a few more minutes, and then went below.

When Beorn came up, I put the professor's proposal to him. He grunted like a great bear when he heard and then, for a moment or two was silent. Then, to my considerable surprise, he nodded his shaggy head. "Ya," he said, with a touch of amusement in his voice, "if the professor wishes it so, we will do it."

I was relieved. Beorn was now looking back toward the open sea, "The weather will change soon," he rumbled.

"It couldn't be much better than it is," I said, going below through the main hatch.

"Is true," he said behind me, "but it could be worse, ya?"

"I guess so," I said. But it was an absent reply; I was still hearing the professor's voice and thinking of the odd note of humor in Beorn's voice when he agreed to sail at night. What was so damned funny?

In the morning I told the professor of our decision, and immediately he became more cheerful. Dot was more questioning.

"Are you sure this is wise, Lute?"

I shrugged, "It's a fifty-fifty sort of deal. We cover more ground but can't cover it as well."

She looked aft, where Beorn sat at the tiller, "What does Beorn say?"

"He agreed to the idea, and he seemed to find it a trifle amusing for some reason."

"Amusing? Why?"

"I don't know. It's his coastline more than mine, and I'm

glad he's not worried about going aground or hitting a rock, but I'm damned if I know why he was amused."

She looked at him and her lips were touched with a smile, "He's the strangest man I ever met."

"And the most dangerous," I said. "Remember the greeting he gave me in your room? He could tear an ox in two if he tried."

"I remember." She touched her hand lightly to the place on her head where he'd struck her. "But look at the way he holds the tiller: like he would hold a bird; hard enough to contain it but not so hard that he might crush it." Her eyes were wide behind her glasses, and I wondered what she was thinking as she watched him.

Whatever Beorn was thinking, it wasn't of her. He was looking off to the northwest, where the sea was rolling down before the wind, and whatever humor I'd seen in his face the night before was no longer there. Rather, his expression was thoughtful and grave. I followed his eyes with mine and could see nothing out of the ordinary: only the deep blue of water reaching to the horizon and the white flecks of foam and spume that capped the waves.

"What is it, Beorn?" I asked, going to him.

"I am not sure. The air is strange. Something is out there over the horizon, I think."

"A storm?"

He shrugged, "The North Sea is there, and storms come out of it. The weather is changing, but I am not sure what it will become. We will be watchful, yes?"

I stood and looked to the northwest. Nothing. I tried to feel the air as he was feeling it, to detect any change in moisture or velocity. Again nothing. I lacked his genius.

"When will it come?" I asked.

He rumbled in discontent, "I cannot tell, Luther. Tomorrow perhaps, perhaps later."

"Not today."

"No."

I looked toward the coast. A few miles ahead I could see a headland jutting into the sea. "Over there, Beorn. Is there an island lying low there, offshore?"

"We will see," he said, and put the tiller over.

An hour later we crossed in front of the headland and saw that it was not the place we sought. There was a low mound of rocks lying off the point, but neither an island worthy of the name nor another headland to the north. Our momentary excitement gone, we bore on up the coast toward a scattering of offshore islands ahead. It was noon when we reached them, and we spent the rest of the day passing among them over shoal water and working our way north.

We split watches during the night and sailed steadily, once bearing in to look at a cliff that shone like a Rembrandt painting in the half-light, finding nothing, and bearing away again. The next morning both Dot and her uncle were dark-eyed, so I sent them below while Beorn and I stayed on deck.

Off to the north, the horizon trembled against the sky and the wind came down cold and clear. There was a chop to the waves and the beginning of a long swell under them. Beorn reached a hand overboard and felt the water.

"Colder," he said. "Until you have seen a North Sea storm from the Arctic, you have seen no storm at all. We must look for a harbor soon or get farther out to sea. I do not like it this close to a lee shore."

I immediately began to worry. If Beorn was disturbed by the prospect of a storm, serious trouble was on the way.

"How long do we have?"

"I do not know," he muttered uncomfortably.

I went below and got the charts and brought them up. We needed a harbor very soon.

But I found nothing near to us.

I touched the chart with my finger, "There is a fiord ahead of us about ten miles, Beorn, but that's the nearest thing. The only other place I can see is about thirty miles back down the coast."

"That last would take us too long," he replied. "This boat would take many hours to get there, even before the wind."

"The fiord ahead, then?"

He frowned to the north, "We will try. Look." A low line of blackness now lay on the northwest horizon like a line of india ink. As I watched, it grew thicker.

"Put up sail," said Beorn, "we will need it."

I shouted below and went forward to shake out the big jib. The professor and Dot stumbled on deck and hurried forward to lend a hand. In ten minutes the *Gate of Horn* was carrying all of her canvas and driving ahead close-hauled. For the first time since I'd seen her, I wished she was faster. The professor shared my thoughts, "She seems to be creeping," he said worriedly.

"You'd better get below and stow things away," I said. "It's going to get bumpy and sloppy before we get to harbor, and the inside of a boat can get smashed up pretty badly if everything isn't fastened down."

"Yes," he said, looking startled. "Come, Dottie." The two of them went below and soon I heard the sounds of locker doors shutting as they began securing the cabin.

The wind rose suddenly and heeled the boat. She immediately picked up speed, and spume began to splat back at us from the bow.

"What do you think, Beorn?" I asked as I slid into the cockpit.

"It will be a close thing," he answered. "The clouds are coming fast and we are sailing into them."

"Damnation! Shall I start the auxiliary?"

He shook his head, and his long hair blew out from beneath his woolen cap, "No. The engine will give us no more speed. It is good only for power."

The wind was picking up rapidly now, and the waves were beginning to rise in front of the fast coming clouds. The horizon, so clear a short time before, had now disappeared into blackness, and far to the windward I could see the gray-black slant of wind-driven rain. I shivered suddenly, and pulled the hood of my parka over my head. Looking at Beorn, I saw him do the same.

"An arctic storm," he called through the wind. "It has blown over half the world to get here. It has come across the ice caps, through the Skagerrak, and down onto us. There is nothing to stop it!"

Our lee rail dipped and began to split the water. The spume mounted over the bow and flew in our faces. Below I heard a clatter of falling tinware and the fuss of someone trying to collect it and get it stowed away before it fell again. Everything on the port side of the boat was now three feet higher than that on the lee side and threatened to go sliding down to starboard.

Half an hour later I felt the first touch of rain. By the time Beorn and I were in our oilskins, the rain had turned to sleet with spits of snow mixed with it. The wind was high and cold, and the sea was mounting. The *Gate of Horn* began to roll and pitch, and it was obvious that we were carrying too much canvas. I yelled to Dot and the professor and the three of us managed to get the storm sails up and the rest stowed in the sail locker. The halyards and sheets were like icy snakes; cold and slippery, they whipped in the wind and slapped at our arms and hands. Dot came forward through a wave of spume and water that broke across the bow and helped haul the last lines tight. The *Gate of Horn* steadied a bit.

In the cockpit, the professor shouted, "How long do these storms last?"

"Different times," bellowed Beorn in reply. "Three days, maybe. Not more than that, I think!"

"My God," cried the professor, "I can't afford three days!"

"Better that than your life!" shouted Dot.

Ahead of us, the shoreline was becoming indistinct. Everything was turning gray and black in the sleet and wind, and our visibility was decreasing rapidly. The howl of wind and sea and the groan of rigging filled our ears, and we were soaked to the skin in spite of our oilskins. Only the oily woolen sweater I wore kept in my body heat.

"Go below and get into heavy clothes," I yelled to Dot and her uncle, who were both pale with cold and wet. "Put on wool, and stay below, if you want to be warm."

With chattering teeth, they did as I asked, and I shut the main hatch behind them. The cockpit was sloshing with water that had come over the side. The water splashed from scupper to scupper, running out no faster than more came in.

The fog thickened and the wind rose. Somewhere in the grayness ahead of us we could hear the roar of surf. Beorn suddenly shouted at me:

"Luther, this is not good! That fiord is too narrow to find in such weather as this! We will go in no farther!"

"It can't be far from here!" I shouted back, straining my eyes ahead through the driving sleet.

"No! Feel the boat! She is riding in shallow water even now. Do you feel it? We are near shoals; we must come about and beat to sea! In deep water we can ride out the storm; here we will perish!"

I could sense something different in the way the boat was riding, but would not have known that it was because she was in shallow water. Then, a hundred feet ahead of us I saw a wave suddenly flash high into the air and break into flying spume. It had broken on a rock or shoal, and beyond it

I could suddenly see surf breaking in long irregular lines upon an unseen shore! We were headed right for it.

"Come about!" I shouted. The *Gate of Horn* lifted on a crest and seemed to fly toward the breaking surf. But Beorn did not lose a second; at the first sound of my cry, he put the tiller down and swung our bow up into the wind. I tore at the jib sheets, got them loose, and winched them down on the other side as we slammed around and caught the wind on the starboard tack. The booms arched across and crashed hard as the sheets caught them. For a moment the boat hung suspended on a wavetop; then, in a shower of spray she beat into the wind and out to sea. A dozen yards behind us, the water was white with breaking surf.

With our lee rain buried in the water, we thrashed out away from the breakers. The fog swept by in great cold masses, and the sleet slanted down from a black sky into a boiling white sea. Wave after wave crashed across and over us, but we drove on out toward deep water with a prayer that our sails would hold. If we lost our canvas, we would be helpless before the wind and would be driven into the surf or onto the rocks to break up.

CHAPTER 11

The storm blew for three days and got worse as it continued. We blew out our mizzen and two jibs during the first day, but managed to get more sail up each time. Dot and the professor, with safety lines tied around them, were constantly useful. Somehow Dot even managed a pot of lukewarm coffee which we laced with Beorn's black liquor and passed around with cold sandwiches. That coffee was the last warm thing we had; there was no way to cook on the stove, and we ate cold rations for the duration of the storm.

There was no way to sleep on the tossing bunks, and all of us began to ache with fatigue. More worrisome to me was our location. Unable to see either sun or land, I had no idea where we were. We might have been just off the coast, or we might have been well out to sea; I didn't know whether we had blown south or had gained to the northward. "Where are we?" I shouted to Beorn on the second day. But even he did not know.

The fog was thick and driven by the wind, and the whitecaps and sleet were the only breaks in the gray-black crashing about us. All of us had taken a good beating from the storm and were wretchedly tired and worn. The boat was weary, too, although none of us could have known it at the

142

time; in the end, it was a weakened stay that kept us from riding out the blow.

When it happened, Dot and I were forward trying to haul up a new jib to replace one which had just blown out. The wind was roaring and the waves were breaking over the deck as we slithered about entangled in icy, blowing lines and sail. Behind us, the reefed mainsail stretched taut and the mainmast groaned in the wind. Without warning, there was a sound like a rifle shot as the windward stays of the mainmast parted. The cables whistled through the air like scythes, shearing the gaff from the mast and snapping the jib stay above our heads. Immediately, the mainmast, thick and solid though it was, simply ripped in two with a tremendous noise and swept downwind into the sea, carrying sails and lines with it. I had only time to throw Dot face down on the deck as the carnage of rigging swept by us, then I was caught across the chest by a loop of flying line and yanked overboard into the confusion of water and rigging.

The shock of the water drove what little breath I had out of me. My chest was caught tight in the loop of line, and I was enmeshed in a thrashing tangle of rope, splintered wood, and torn canvas that trailed off the *Gate of Horn*. Above the roaring all about me I heard Dot scream something to Beorn and then saw him rise in the cockpit, lean out, and sweep a long arm out for me as I was carried aft past the boat's stern. I got an arm up and hooked hands with him; then, with a rolling heave, he hauled me over the side into the cockpit. In another moment his knife flashed in his hand and he had slashed away the loop of line that had taken me overboard. Half conscious, I lay in the bottom of the cockpit and heard him shout to the professor to get the ax and cut away the wreckage.

My mind was confused, and there was a great pain across my chest and in my left knee; I could hear the sound of the ax chopping and a bit later felt the boat, which had been taking a terrible battering as she drifted broadside to the waves, entangled in the broken rigging that hung alongside, rise a bit and seem to shake herself.

"She's free," I heard the professor call.

"Take the tiller while I get the engine started," roared Beorn.

Then Dot was beside me with a bottle of scotch. To hell with Uncle Cyril, I thought, and took a long pull. Dot took the bottle back and looked into my face. She could see pain there, I suppose, for she immediately set about getting me below. Beorn, seeing her intention, lifted me down through the hatch and put me on a bunk. Then he went back to the engine.

"Can you tell if anything's broken?" asked Dot.

"No," I said, "I may have a couple of cracked ribs, or I may not. Look at my left knee, though, and see if I broke that. I gave it a good bang somewhere along the line."

Her long fingers went over the leg with cool detachment. "I can't tell," she said finally. "You may have cracked something, or you may have just a sprain. In either case, your knee is swelling and you won't be doing much walking for a while."

The engine started then, and so I didn't ask if it was all right for me to swim.

"Leave me the scotch," I said, instead.

With the engine going, I wasn't too worried about staying afloat, but later the wind mounted and we began to blow back toward the coast. The engine ground away steadily but was no match for the storm; without sail, the *Gate of Horn* simply could not gain to windward or even keep the gains she already had; slowly yet inexorably we were driven stern-first toward land. Fog and sleet blinded us, and when the third night of the storm came, making darker that which

was already gray-black and cold, we were completely helpless.

Beorn came down and sat with me a moment to explain
why he wasn't running before the wind.

"Is not smart," he said. "I do not know where I am in this
sea. If I run downwind, I will hit . . . what? . . . open
water? Rocks? I do not know, Luther. Besides, is three days
now that this storm has blown. Soon it will be over, yes?
Better, I think, for us to fight the wind here, than to run
from it."

It made sense, and I was glad he'd come down to tell
me. Before he went up on deck, he opened his locker and
gave me a pull from his private stock. The dark liquor hit
my middle like fire and drove the pain of my chest and knee
far enough away from my consciousness so that I was almost comfortable when Beorn went back on deck. Five
hours later the eastern sky brightened just enough for us to
see breakers behind us.

Desperately, Beorn turned the throttle as high as it would
go and tried to clear us off into deep water. But it was no
good; the boat gained nothing to the windward and lost
only a slight part of her previous drift. It was obvious that
we were about to be driven onto the shore and pounded to
pieces in the surf. Dot came down in time to help me into a
life jacket and get me on deck. My leg hurt like hell, but
did help support part of my weight. I wanted no part of being below when we hit.

On deck I could see much better. I looked astern at the
breakers and was surpsised to see no beach or rocks.

"What's the water breaking on?" I shouted to Beorn.

He shook his head and pointed first left and then right. I
followed his gesture with my eyes and saw the grimness of
our position. Both to left and to right, land masses loomed
dimly through the driving sleet and fog. Ragged, rock-
broken cliffs thrust into the sea on either side of us, prevent-

ing us from turning across the wind and seeking out some break in the surf. Between these cliffs the water was bursting in white geysers over some hidden rocks or shoals, and it was toward these breakers that the *Gate of Horn* was being carried. No solid land could be seen behind the breakers; there was only a swirl of fog and indistinct gray-black spirals of foam and mist.

"We're going to hit!" roared Beorn. "Stay with the boat as long as you can. She may stay together even though she's beached! Tie yourself to the boat if you can; you'll be safer on board than in the water!"

We had little more time. I peered astern, trying to see some break in the surf that we might head for, but I saw nothing. The swells were riding high over some unseen thing in their path and were breaking in a fury as they hit it. Spray was flying thirty feet into the air before being swept away by the wind.

"Beorn," I shouted, "put us about and let's ride a wave up as high as we can go on those rocks!" It was the best thing I could see for us to do. If we could ride a high wave far up on the rocks, we stood a better chance of keeping the boat in one piece until the storm blew out.

"Ya!" Beorn thundered. "Is the best thing, I think!"

He timed his turn perfectly, slewing off broadside to the waves with the propeller well in the water, then letting a wave catch the bow and spin us around until we were pointed right toward the wall of breakers. Mist and spray were so thick that I could see practically nothing. Beorn played with the engine, inching in toward the surf as he watched it break, and watching astern for the wave he wanted to catch and ride in.

At last it came, a great rolling growler five feet higher than its fellows that came down on us out of the mist. Just before it passed under us, Beorn threw the shift forward and put the accelerator full up. The *Gate of Horn* leaped ahead

toward the breakers just as the wave caught and lifted our
stern. Then, like a surfboarder, Beorn rode the boat in on the
wave. We were borne along like a leaf for a moment, and
then were engulfed in a solid sheet of water and roaring
sound.

Something smashed at the boat's undersides, and the
jolt of it sent me sprawling across the cockpit. The *Gate of
Horn* lifted and crashed down once more, and I saw the
mizzen mast snap in two and carry away over the side.
Water burst over the side of the boat and poured into the
cockpit and down the hatch into the cabin. There was a
rending roar of tortured wood, a sudden sideways slither,
and sudden calmness. The roar of water and wind was all
around us, but the boat itself lay bobbing in calm water.

I pulled myself up from the cockpit floor, choking out a
mouthful of water, and looked around us. Beorn too was
looking about with an odd expression of wonder.

"What's happened?" It was Dot's voice from somewhere
forward. I turned and saw her and the professor sitting
dazedly on the foredeck looking about at their surround-
ings.

"We've crossed a reef, or something like a reef," I said,
beginning to see things more clearly. "We're on the lee side,
away from the storm and we're in some sort of harbor." On
both left and right the cliffs we'd seen from beyond the
breakers could still be seen, and now I could see still another rising cliff farther downwind, on the other side of the
bay we were in.

Beorn saw the land downwind too, and was quick to
get anchors over so we wouldn't be blown down onto that
shore. Then he went below to check for damage. In the sleet,
fog, and strangely quiet water, the rest of us payed out
anchor line until we came under the lee of the land mass on
our port side. There the boat bobbed gently in the water.
She was terrible to behold, with her masts gone and her

deck a mass of splintered timbers and tangled rigging, but she was afloat and riding easily. Beorn came up from below and announced that we had leaks along the keel, but that hand pumps could handle the water easily. When I heard that, I sat down rather heavily. We were beaten up a bit, but were still alive and free from serious damage.

I was looking around for Dot's bottle of scotch when I first became aware of an odd silence on the boat. I looked up and saw that the professor and Dot were staring about as if in a trance. The babble of conversation that had followed our realization that we were safe had died away, and they were peering around through the fog in silent wonder. I followed their gazes, wondering what it was that entranced them.

The morning sun was climbing slowly into the southern sky, and was sending its rays through the fog and sleet. As the light increased, gaps in the fog appeared, held, and disappeared again as the wind swept the mist to the south. Through the holes in the fog I could finally see where we were: We lay in an oddly shaped inlet between two tall, rocky headlands. To our left, as the *Gate of Horn* tugged gently at her anchor, rose another land mass that could only be an island.

The professor's shout of joy and disbelief echoed oddly in the fog, and even as it did, I recognized the reality behind the chart: We were lying in the lee of Beowulf's island, under the headlands where the warrior king had fought his last battle and been buried.

CHAPTER 12

The morning was chaotic, and we could scarcely contain the professor on board the boat. He was like a child, desperate to get onto the island; only the fact that the dinghy had been damaged kept him aboard. While Beorn worked on the dinghy, the professor ran about the deck with his camera and took pictures of the rain- and fog-shrouded cliffs. "Marvelous," he kept repeating.

By afternoon the fog began to blow away and we could finally see what had happened to us. Between the island and the northernmost of the two headlands was a sand bar which the professor immediately identified as the "bridge" on his chart. It was on this shoal that we'd seen the surf bursting, and over the shoal that we'd ridden the *Gate of Horn*. Once in the lee of the sand spit, the water had become almost calm and we had been able to anchor in the island's lee. Lucky for us, the tide had been high.

"The dinghy is ready now," said Beorn at last, putting aside his tools and sliding the little boat over the side. The professor dashed below, battled his way through the equipment strewn cabin, and reappeared with a small pickax.

"Come, everybody," he called, "let us all go ashore together!"

But Beorn was more concerned with his boat than with

the island, and my knee was too weak to allow me to walk around. Dot and her uncle, therefore, got in the dinghy and rowed ashore. From the cockpit I took pictures of them as they rowed in and landed; good stuff for the future book. First landing on Beowulf's Island; big *National Geographic* spread; fantasy.

They waved to us from the tiny beach and started inland; in a moment they were out of sight. Beorn looked after them in silence, then grunted like an old bear and started clearing up the decks. Salvable line and fittings he piled forward near the sail locker; everything else went overboard and soon sank or drifted away downwind. Unable to help, I settled back and drank scotch with a feeling of heady abandon.

When the decks were cleared away, Beorn went below to begin cleaning there. Things were messier inside than out, for when the *Gate of Horn* had come over the shoal she'd taken a couple of bad jolts that had shaken everything from the lockers out into one tangled heap on the floor. Food was mixed with papers and tackle; a bottle of cooking oil had broken and run across a bunk, and there was a layer of broken glass and strawberry jam over everything. Beorn started patiently to sort things out, clean them up, and stow them away in their proper places. He seemed oddly uncurious about the island or what Dot and her uncle might find there.

It was dusk before the two explorers came back. The dinghy had scarcely thumped alongside the *Gate of Horn* before the two of them were on deck ablaze with excitement.

"Luther, Beorn!" they cried to us. "Calm down, calm down," they said to each other. "You should see it!" they said to us.

"Tell us all about it," I said. And together they did.

The chart was remarkably accurate. The island was pear-shaped and had a high point on the western, ocean, side upon which they had found the remains of what might once have been a watchtower where a sharp-eyed Geat could look far to sea and spy enemy ships coming. On the northern and southern sides of the island, ragged cliffs and rocks ran down to the sea and made landings impossible or at least totally unfeasible. Anyone attempting to land there would either be broken on the rocks or, having survived them, would be faced with a fifty- to four-hundred-foot climb up a cliff at the top of which defenders would be waiting with stones and, possibly, hot oil.

The only landing place was that small stretch of beach on the eastern side of the island where the dinghy had landed. And any vessel coming in to land there would have to pass first through a narrow gut of water between the southernmost of the two headlands and the cliffs of the island.

"The channel is only a hundred feet or so wide," the professor said, with a thrill to his voice. "It runs from the ocean up into the fiord behind the island in a northeast direction. Any boat coming in there would be cut off from all but a southwest wind and would probably be forced to row in. With her men rowing, she would be at less than full preparedness for attack. If the Geats had an armed ship waiting just inside the fiord, they could strike the enemy a fatal blow while he was still at his oars.

"And on the top of the island's cliffs, above the channel, we found piles of throwing stones. That suggests that the Geats had catapults there, guarding the channel. Any enemy boat that came through could be smashed to pieces!"

The island was a natural fortress, upon which a few good fighting men could stand off tremendous odds. How the Geats must have rejoiced at finding such a place.

"We found two fresh springs," Dottie cried. "The water is cold and good, and there seems to be plenty for a good-sized town. If the island were sieged, the islanders could hold out for months—as long as their food would let them. And they could even fish without much danger and add to their diet that way!"

I'd never seen her so animated; she seemed almost child-like in her excitement, and her enthusiasm was infectious. Beorn looked at her with an expression of pure delight.

"Remember the chart?" said the professor. "The inscription there that read '. . . an ancient people built high walls here before they perished'? We can't be sure yet, but I think we've discovered who those people were. Between the bridge over there and the ruins of the city we found inland there are the remains of a roadway. Now neither Dottie nor I is a classicist, but both of us are sure the road is Roman! It looks very similar to the old Roman roads that still exist in England; the construction is the same!"

"Think of that," exclaimed Dot. "If we're right, it will mean that at least one Roman party settled here in the early days of the Christian era, possibly in an effort at colonization similar to the one made in Britain. If we can find more evidence, and I'm sure we can, we stand on the brink of a very important discovery!"

"And what, for my purposes, is more important," said the professor, his eyes gleaming behind his glasses, "is the fact that this island and those headlands back there, if they hide the barrow and the tomb as I believe they do, prove that I have been right." He blinked his eyes and shook his head as if to clear it of cobwebs, and when he spoke again his voice was shaking. "The prospect is stupefying."

Stupefying indeed. As the darkness deepened around us, and the storm continued to blow itself out, Beorn got the galley cleaned up enough for us to have a hot meal. Dot and her uncle talked about the island while Beorn and I chewed and listened, in rare good humor at their excitement. Dot was bright with her eyes, words, and laughter, and I felt myself drawn toward her. After supper, she and the professor rushed to write down their observations of the day. Written records would, in the final analysis, be more important than verbal reports. While they worked below, I sat in the cockpit sipping scotch and looking at the dimly lighted island. Beside me, Beorn was silent, thinking thoughts I could not guess. His eyes were veiled by darkness, and he puffed his ancient pipe like some creature of another time.

The next day I went ashore with the others and cut a cane from a growth of scrub. Beorn and the others, carrying shovels, pickaxes, and sifting screens went directly inland to the ruins of the city, but I hobbled off on my own, promising to join them later.

I found the road first, and followed it down toward the sand bar we'd ridden over during the storm. Now, at low tide and hours after the storm had passed to the south, the water rolled in between the island and the headland on the shore with scarcely a ripple. A block or two of stone jutted above the water about fifty yards from the island's beach. I sat down and took off my shoes and then inched, limping, into the water. It was cold!

Walking carefully and using my cane, I waded out toward the stones; fifty feet from the beach, the water was still only about eighteen inches deep. When I reached the stones, I'd gotten wet only halfway up my thighs. I sat down on one of the stones and rested while I examined it. It was so worn by water that I could not tell whether it was natural or had been placed there by human hands. I was about halfway to the mainland shore, so I went on across; nowhere was the water deeper than midway on my thighs. I splashed up onto the Swedish shore with blue legs and freezing feet, and turned to look back at the island. From my vantage point there was no way to tell that a sand bar existed. A stranger to the place would never guess that he could walk across to the island.

I walked across the narrow beach at the foot of the headland, looking for a sign of the road; but I found nothing. If there had ever been a road on this side, it was long since overgrown, washed away, or covered by sliding earth and stone from the headland. I stopped hunting and looked up at the jutting cliffs above me. Somewhere up there or over on the headland across the fiord to the south we should find signs of the dragon's barrow or of the tomb. If the professor's theory was correct.

Above me, the headland rose hundreds of feet into the air, splitting the sea wind, its top still touched with wisps of fog. It was huge and old, and tangled with trees and ground cover between its layers of broken granite. Juts and rims of rock broke out of the foliage and created giant, ragged steps up to the top. Here and there, sheer cliffs fell down toward me, their stony faces still wet from the storm.

Finding anything up there would not be simple. A barrow, if there was one, could be anywhere on that vast, broken face, and would be hidden by a thousand years' erosion and overgrowth. We had our work cut out for us, and I, with my fat, aching knee, was in no shape to be much help. If anything up there was to be found, it would be found by Dot, Beorn, and Uncle Cyril.

I walked back across the beach and into the water. When I reached the rocks, I turned and moved parallel to the beaches for a few steps. Almost immediately, the water deepened, inching up toward my waist. I turned and crossed the other way; again after a few steps my feet began to slip out in front of me and the water lapped at my hips. I backed up, pushing with my cane, until I regained shallower water. I'd found out what I wanted to know: the sand bar was about ten feet wide, and dropped off sharply on either side into deep water. At low tide, and as long as a man stayed on the sand bar, he could cross easily. However, a man weighed down with armor and weapons, and unfamiliar with the "bridge," could, in the heat of battle, easily slip off into deep water and drown. It was a perfect defensive barrier: no trouble to those who knew its secret, but impossible for those who didn't.

I walked on across to the island, put my shoes back on, and lit a cigarette. By the time I'd finished a third cigarette, I began to see what I was looking for: The water was beginning to move across the sand bar and rise on the rocks out in the channel. I watched as the water rose and began to flow faster over the bridge. After another half hour I got to my feet and went to look for the others. My admiration for the defenders of the island was considerable. Not only was the sand bar almost impervious to attackers at low tide, but it was probably completely unusable except for an hour or two at dead low tide. At all other times, the water would be too deep and swift moving for anyone to cross over. And in addition, the sand bar created a bit of a rip during rising and falling tide which would make crossing by boat very hazardous. Unless the oarsmen of such a boat were strong and knowledgeable, the current would spin them past the tiny beach where the road led to the sand bar and would bring them under the cliffs where Dot and the professor had found the catapult stones. Once there, no boat would have a chance.

I walked along the ancient road toward the ruins of the city. The roadway was greatly overgrown with grass and shrubs, and the stones which had formed its pavement were often broken or tumbled into piles by roots or frost swells. There was a timeless quality about it that fascinated me; it was as if I could feel the thrust of antiquity beneath my feet as the old stones received and released my steps. Nearing the top of a small rise, I passed between two marker stones, one of which had fallen and was half covered by vines. Beyond the stones I came to the top of the hill and could see the city itself.

It didn't look like much to me, but then I'm no archeologist. There were broken remnants of a few stone walls, many overgrown mounds of earth, and some squared-off humps that might once have been building foundations. Beorn, Dot, and the professor were working with their tools at one of the mounds. Dot looked up and saw me and waved excitedly. Too far away to see what they were really doing, I waved back and limped toward them. When I got closer, Dot ran to meet me. In her hand she held a familiar looking dark disk.

"What's this?" I asked, taking it in my hand.

Her eyes blazed, "That's a gold coin, a Roman coin! Look at it carefully and you can see the markings. We found it in a little stone box. Luther, Uncle Cyril was right. This was a Roman city before the Geats ever settled here!"

"Great," I said. I bounced the coin thoughtfully in my hand before giving it back to her.

* *

Four days later, all of us had gotten over the initial thrill of discovering the island. The professor and Beorn were digging carefully down through a mound of earth. From the mound they extracted and set aside whatever they found: bits of broken pottery, bones, scraps of mortar, and an occasional hand-fashioned tool. They were careful not to break anything, and limited the size of their excavation to a pit about three feet by three feet square. Four other pits of similar size, each about four feet deep, had been dug at different spots around the ruin of the city. Loose dirt had been sifted and piled beside each excavation, and a small collection of knickknacks had already been gathered and put aboard the *Gate of Horn*. Uncle Cyril was being very systematic.

In the pit, the professor stopped digging. He climbed

out, wiping perspiration from his brow, and walked over to where Dot and I sat. He lit a cigarette, and Beorn came to join us.

"One thing is obvious," said the professor, "and that is that we will need a much larger group of people to excavate this place properly. I wish now that I knew more of archeology, but unhappily I do not."

"We have done well, I think," rumbled Beorn mildly. "We have found much of interest, ya?"

"Yes, Beorn," smiled the professor, "but it is nothing compared to what still waits to be found. If we can get a large group of qualified people here, we can find things that might well astound the world." He turned to me, "Beorn is correct, though, in saying that we have found much of interest. Specifically we've found both Roman relics and relics I presume to be Geatish. The Roman remains lie under those of the Geats, proving that the Geats were latecomers to the island just as the chart suggests.

"With trained men and proper equipment, a great deal can be learned here. Knowledge, for example, that a Roman colony of a certain size existed here for, say, fifty years during the third century A.D. and that a Geatish fortress was then established between year X and year Y would give us considerable added insight into matters involved with trade, war, and the social structure of those times." He paused and looked up at the headlands, "But now, I believe, it is time for the four of us to turn our attention elsewhere. We have gathered enough remains from these diggings, and have enough photographic evidence and written commentary to convince anyone of the value of our find, and of the validity of my theory concerning this site. I believe that the island had best be left now to more knowledgeable hands than ours, although I of course will want to be part of that archeological work when it does begin."

"And me?" I asked, not anxious, suddenly, to have such a project take place without me.

Uncle Cyril looked at me with cautious eyes, "Why yes, Luther, you will come too, if you wish. After all, it was through your efforts that we got here in the first place."

"Good," I said, thinking behind the cover of my words. "A Master's thesis about these diggings might be interesting."

"It might indeed," he said. "Of course I plan to produce a paper of my own very shortly." His eyes glinted coolly behind his glasses.

"Of course, sir," I said quickly. Until I was safely back on Weststock's academic roles I needed the ungrateful old bastard more than he now needed me.

Dot flipped the coin and caught it in her hand, "Too bad we found only one of these," she laughed. "With a box of them we could finance our own expedition."

"We'll find few of those, my dear," said her uncle. "We were fortunate to have found even that one." He turned then and looked up at the headlands, "Unless we find some up there."

"The tomb." Dot's voice was bright.

Beorn seemed suddenly awkward and uncomfortable, "Is unwise to disturb the dead," he said. His mouth twitched into what seemed almost a smile, then turned down and back to blankness.

The professor gestured impatiently, "We have little time left before the summer ends, and we must learn if the barrow and tomb are there! Tomorrow we'll cross over to the mainland and go up those headlands."

Beorn's eyes were fathomless as we collected our tools and artifacts and started back to the camp we had set up near the beach.

That night, while Dot and the professor were writing down their documentation of the day's discoveries, I noted with annoyance that my knee, which had been improving steadily, was beginning to swell again. By morning it was fat and painful, and so when the others left to go up the mountain, I stayed behind in the island camp.

"Come," Beorn had said to the others, "we must cross the bridge now, while the tide is low."

"Do be careful, Lute," said Dot. "I'm sorry you can't come too."

"Be careful," I said, "and good hunting."

I sat and watched them walk off down the old road toward the sand bar. There, Beorn had them remove their shoes and then led them into the water, out past the rocks, and up onto the far shore. With the field glasses I watched them start up the slope on the far side. When they went into the first of the trees and I could no longer see them, I sat back, got out a cigarette, and wondered how Beorn knew enough about the sand bar to lead them so confidently across.

As far as I knew, I was the only one of us who had taken time to study the bridge and to walk it at low tide. I tried to remember if I'd told anyone of my trip across the sand bar, but could not recall having mentioned it. Strange.

Beorn had behaved a bit oddly for several days now. He did not, for one thing, seem to be particularly excited by what we'd found on the island; on the other hand, he seemed genuinely interested in the professor's interpretation of the meaning of the relics, and seemed to gain from them some meaningful understanding of the past. The professor's interpretation of the island was more novel and interesting to him than the island itself. In addition, the island had made Beorn much more open in his appreciation of Dottie, and he was becoming almost unconcerned about whether any of us noticed it or not. The fact that I was the only one who *did* seem to notice it was doubly annoying. Dottie didn't even know that he was eying her like a hungry bear. A final oddity in Beorn's behavior, however, disturbed me more than any of the others: He didn't seem very worried about his boat.

None of us could know how far we were from any village where we might get help in repairing the *Gate of Horn*. With both masts gone, along with lines, stays, fitting, and canvas, we were dependent solely on the motor and whatever remained of our gas supply to get us out and back to civilization. Beorn, if he were anything like me, should have been worrying about this, perhaps working to rig a jury rig of some sort so we could at least get down the coast to the nearest town. But instead he gave no sign of worry or concern. His only work, once he'd checked the motor and propeller and found them both functionable, was to go aboard the boat once a day and pump out her bilges with his hand pump. Aside from that he did nothing.

I was perplexed.

But I had other problems to worry about. I didn't know where we were, and I wanted to find out. Pushing myself up with my cane, I limped down to the dinghy and rowed out to the boat. On board I found my sextant and shot the sun, marking down the sighting and figures in my journal. The professor, when he thought of it, would want to know our exact position, and when he asked I would now be able to supply him with precise figures. I scribbled out latitude and longitude on two pieces of paper, one for him and one for me. In the stillness of the sheltered fiord, I'd gotten good sights on the sun and was sure, finally, that I had gotten my fix precisely.

I put the sextant back in its case, sat, and drank some of the professor's scotch. I thought of Beorn. In my mind I could see him moving across this ancient land, ax in hand, seeking dragons. Above the cabin door hung the rifle I'd seen the first day I'd come aboard in Boston harbor. Once or twice we'd shot sharks with it on our way across the

Atlantic. Beorn didn't like sharks particularly, and had no objection to my shooting them when they came near the boat and circled us.

Now, feeling like a fool, I considered taking the rifle back to camp with me. But that was foolish. I had no reason to take it, and it was too big to hide. Everyone would see it there and would ask why. And what would I say? Should I say, "Well, as I was sitting out there drinking scotch, I got this picture in my mind of Beorn moving through the woods with an ax in his hand, and he looked like one of those old Geats himself, so I brought this rifle back to protect myself."

Still, like others I've known, I'm generally unwilling to forget my most irrational forebodings, so I humped myself over to Beorn's locker, opened it, dug around, and came up with the Luger pistol I'd found there before. It was heavy in my hand but a hell of a lot easier to conceal than a rifle. I popped the magazine out, saw that it was fully loaded, checked to see that there was no shell in the firing chamber, and slapped the magazine back into the handle.

With the pistol making a bit of a lump under my belt and sweater, I gimped back on deck, got into the dinghy, and rowed ashore. At camp I stuffed the pistol into my duffel bag, relieved that I no longer had it on my person, and sat down with my glasses to watch the headlands and wait for the others to return.

CHAPTER 13

Late in the afternoon I saw them come out of the trees at the foot of the headland. The tide was still too high for them to come across, so I could only watch them through the glasses as they waved excitedly and shouted words I could not hear across the channel. Finally, after I had joylessly smoked half a pack of cigarettes, they came across and bounded happily into camp. It was obvious that their news was good.

"Amazing luck," crowed Uncle Cyril.

"Fantastic," echoed Dottie. She waved her camera. "I've got some great shots of it!"

"What? What?" I shouted into the babble of voices. "What did you find?"

"A burial place of the old people," boomed Beorn, his voice not without enthusiasm.

"I'm sure it's the Dragon's Barrow," said the professor. "Everything matches the description in the poem. The barrow is near the top of the headland, better hidden but not unlike extant barrows that have been found elsewhere in northern Europe. When we went up, then, we simply paid no attention to the lower or middle portions of the mountain, but went directly to the top. It was a gamble, but it paid off handsomely. Even though we limited our search area, there was a huge portion of the headland to cover, and when we found the barrow it was, finally, almost by chance." He looked at Dot and Beorn. "Don't you agree?"

"Ya, there was some luck," nodded Beorn, "but because of you, we were looking in the right place for such luck to happen." He looked at the professor with admiration.

Dot interrupted, "It was almost a matter of logic. We presumed that the poem was accurate and that the barrow, if it was there, would be similar to others that have been found here, in England, and elsewhere. So we looked where it ought to be, and nowhere else. And we knew—or at least Uncle Cyril knew—what sort of building materials would have to be moved into place by anyone who built such a barrow. Knowing that, we could ignore portions of our search area that seemed unlikely from a builder's standpoint and concentrate on areas that seemed more likely."

"And even so, we were simply lucky in the end," said the professor. "Beorn here took a little trip of his own between two rimrocks and found the opening." He looked warmly at Beorn.

"I knew it from what you had told me," Beorn rumbled awkwardly.

"You have marvelous eyes," cried Dot. "I never would have seen it." Again Beorn looked awkward, and Dot swept her bright myopic eyes toward me. "The entrance has fallen in, and everything is overgrown with vines and underbrush. Beorn saw it, though, and called to us!"

"What did you find inside?" I finally managed to ask. There was a short pause.

"Ah," said the professor finally. "Nothing at all."

"Nothing?" It was quite anticlimactic.

"The entrance was filled with fallen stone and dirt. We got only about twenty feet into the tunnel when our way was blocked. We'll have to wait for more men and equipment before excavating. But that makes no difference, if the poem is correct, for the barrow will be empty anyway, its treasure having been removed by Beowulf's followers and placed in the burial tower. We did get far enough in to identify the barrow as being characteristic of known barrows of that era." The professor's face was eager. "The burial tower is what is important now, and is what we shall seek out tomorrow on the other headland. If we find it, we will have everything we've sought for! Everything!"

"Treasure?"

"My God, man, this whole place is treasure! The burial tower will be the final proof we need to get all the backing we'll ever want or need. When we come back here again, we'll be a hundred men, and not just a motley crew of four!"

"It's wonderful!" cried Dot, letting her scholastic defenses completely down.

Off to her left, Beorn looked at her from beneath his bristling brows, and let excitement seep from him in spite of his stoicism.

I straightened my bad leg and rubbed my hand down across my knee. "Listen," I said, "I've missed everything else on this trip, and I'm damned if I want to miss this last find. I'm going with you tomorrow."

The professor looked at me without sympathy. "We spent most of this morning climbing that headland, and tomorrow's climb will be equally hard. I doubt if your leg will hold up. You will simply slow us down."

"In that case, you'll just be slowed up," I said, "but I intend to be there with you when you get to the top!"

"Oh, Lute," exclaimed Dot, "let's not argue now." She shot silent appeals to both Uncle Cyril and me.

Unexpectedly Beorn spoke. "You will come, Luther. I will walk with you up the mountain. If your leg fails you, I will carry you myself." An enigmatic smile played upon his lips and was gone.

"Thank you, Beorn," I said.

"Oh, Beorn, you are marvelous," said Dot, smiling. She turned to the professor, "You're satisfied, aren't you, Uncle Cyril? Lute won't be slowing us at all now."

"Very well, Luther," he said, "if Beorn is willing to help you, I have no objection to your coming."

"I will help him," rumbled Beorn, "with pleasure. It is right that the captain of the ship should be with his crew at such a time." His eyes twinkled in private humor.

But I was touched by an odd sense of dismay as I looked at him, and could not share his irony. There was some sense of resolution about him that had not been there before. It was as though he had decided on a course of action which had perplexed him before, and was now firm in his mind as to what he must do. The occasional awkwardness I'd seen in him during the past few days was gone. In its place was strength and irony.

Feeling a bit like an ass, I decided to take the Luger with me up the headland in the morning.

The west coast of Sweden is irregular in outline and varied in the face it presents to the sea. In places, the coast is low and smooth; in others it thrusts high and jagged cliffs into the Kattegat. In the clear air of morning, we crossed the fiord behind the island in the dinghy and landed at the base of such a cliff: the southernmost of the two great headlands.

All of us were touched with excitement and were anxious to get up the cliffs. My knee was bound tight in elastic bandages, and I had a walking stick to help me along. The Luger was tucked in my belt, butt forward, under my left arm. My heavy oily sweater covered it quite well.

The others carried light digging equipment: a shovel, pick, crowbar, and a couple of canvas bags for whatever knickknacks we might find. In addition, Dot and the profes-

sor carried cameras and writing materials, and Beorn carried sandwiches, water, a coil of climbing rope, and a flask
of whiskey.

With the dinghy well up on the beach, we started up the
mountain. At first the incline was slight, and we made our
way quite easily, but soon the pitch of the hill became
steeper and our going became slower. There was a tangle of
undergrowth at the base of the cliffs and a tumble of huge
fallen boulders from the rimrocks above. Small stones turned
beneath our feet, and our shoes slipped on wet grass and
dirt which was dampened by a myriad of tiny water seep-
ages under the cliffs. I moved carefully at the tail of the
procession, knowing that I could afford no slips or falls. My
knee seemed fairly strong, but would stand no abuse.

Gradually we climbed above the first layer of trees, and
could look back down onto the island and the boat. Fifteen
hundred years ago, an enemy tribesman looking down like
this would have seen a small fortress-city lying below him
on the island just beyond the reach of his arrows. He would,
if he were wise, content himself with looking, for attack was
suicidal; there was no way for him to enter the fortress.
Looking down now, I again marveled at the genius of the
men who had made their city there and kept it against their
enemies.

We went higher, and began to pass between and over
rims of rock. Once we seemed trapped between two cliffs,
one below and one above us, but we retraced our steps,
took another route and finally topped the higher cliff along
a tiny trail made by some animal that lived among the
rocks. On top of this cliff we took a much-needed breather
and then went on. Twice we seemed stopped by cliffs, but
each time Beorn, muscular as a bear, somehow thrust himself up the walls and pulled the rest of us up with the climbing rope. We climbed higher and higher until, at last we
again were forced to rest. The professor handed me his

binoculars and pointed across the fiord at the opposite head-land.

"There," he said. "See those two rimrocks across from us at almost this same level?"

"Yes."

"Between them is the Dragon's Barrow. Now look to your left, there where that little sandy tableland is formed above the cliff . . ."

I shifted the glasses, "Yes. I see it."

"That is where the battle between the dragon and Beo-wulf took place. Remember the poem? It tells us that the dragon came out and met the old king below the barrow and that they fought there. That level spot is the only place on the front of the headland that is flat enough for such a fight to have taken place. And look below at the cliff. It drops almost directly into the fiord. That too fits the poem when it describes how the warriors rolled the dragon's body down into the sea."

Dot, who sat beside us, pointed to a small cliff above and to the right of the barrow, "Wiglaf might have stood there, don't you think? He must have watched the fight and then gone in to help his king while the others fled."

Beorn spoke unexpectedly, "My father was Wiglaf."

We turned to face him, "Beorn Wiglafson," I said, "of course." I was annoyed that I hadn't thought of it before.

"Wiglaf's son," echoed the professor, looking at Beorn with new interest.

"I knew there was something about you . . ." Dot began. But then her voice died away as if she really had nothing to say at all, and she simply looked at him. I couldn't blame her; he looked as big and old as the headland itself.

"We are an ancient people," he thundered. "We are from this land, and are seafarers and farmers. My father's father was also Wiglaf, and his father before him. My brother who died long ago was Wiglaf." He gestured across the fiord.

"This Wiglaf of whom the poem tells, he is a name in a song my uncle sang when I was a child." He looked at Dot with his great dark eyes. "It was a song of battle between one people and another. . . ." Then suddenly he ceased speaking and got suddenly to his feet, "Come," he growled, "let us go up the mountain."

We looked at him curiously, but he paid us no heed and turned away up the headland. With an exchange of looks, we followed him. It had been an abrupt but interesting conversation.

We climbed higher and higher up the headland until, near the top, we came to the foot of a cliff which rose above us like a wall. I put my hands on it and leaned back, looking up. It was unbroken stone, vertical and unscalable. Wet with sweat, we stared at one another. We were stopped.

"We'll go around it," panted the professor. Beorn grunted something unintelligible, and we began to work our way around the lower edge of the cliff, slithering on fallen rocks and teetering around undergrowth. My knee was beginning to swell again and I was limping in spite of myself, but no one was paying any attention to me. Beorn, who had promised to be my horse, if need be, was instead at the head of our pack working his way eastward along the side of the headland. The rest of us followed.

For nearly half a mile we trailed under the lip of the cliff which rimmed the top of the headland. Then, to our exhausted delight, the rim of rock turned into the mountain and disappeared, leaving only an earthen mountainside for us to scale. With new vigor we climbed up until the hillside began to round off under our feet. Then, with a final burst of energy, we went on until we reached a spot where the earth sloped down both in front and in back of us. We had reached the top of the ridge that ran out to the point of the headland. All of us were out of breath, but no one suggested rest.

"Come along," said the professor, turning westward toward the sea. "We can't be far away now."

Without waiting to see if we were following, he started walking hurriedly along the ridge, skirting undergrowth and ducking under trees. The rest of us followed and soon found ourselves on what seemed to be a pathway. The others took no note of it, but I was slow and limping, and my curiosity was aroused. What was a path doing here?

Or was it a path? It was, after all, only a winding opening through the trees along the ridge. Perhaps, I began to think as I gimped along, it wasn't a path at all, but only a natural break in the vegetation. But then I saw a cut root off to the side.

Interesting. Lifting my eyes from the root, I thought I saw Beorn's face turned toward mine for a fraction of a second. But I could not be sure. He and Dot were ahead, trailing after the professor, and I was trailing after them. I limped on and, knowing now that there were signs to see, saw more subtle signs of human handiwork: a stone rolled out of a narrow spot in the path; a branch broken back.

Ahead, the others quickened their pace as they neared the point of the headland and topped a small rise. For a moment the professor paused while Dot and Beorn came up to him. The trees ended where they stood, but because of the elevation on which they stood, I could see nothing beyond them. Suddenly both Dot and her uncle started to run, and disappeared down out of my sight. A moment later Beorn too bobbed down below my line of vision. Muttering, I loped ahead, my knee throbbing more and more angrily.

When I topped the rise, I found myself looking out on a barren thrust of rock and earth. Behind me, the vegetation ended abruptly, and in front of me the headland ended in the cliff that had stopped us on our ascent from the bottom. On three sides of the barren flat the cliff fell precipitously down, and beyond the point of the headland the Kattegat sparkled blue and white out toward the western horizon. Somewhere out there, beyond the reach of my eyes, lay the northern coast of Jutland!

To the left and right, the rugged coast of Sweden swept away. Broken green, grays, and browns thrust toward the sea as the land jarred out of sight in either direction, each encounter between earth and sea ringed in lines of white surf and waves. Sea birds worked along the wind currents around the cliffs, sounding their raucous cries as they vied for fish and grubs.

I was astonished by the grandeur of it, and it was a long moment before I realized that we had finally come to the end of our search: Out there in front of me, across the barren flat and at the very point of the headland, Dot and the professor were standing at the foot of a broken tower of stone that stood on the lip of the cliff toward the sea.

Beorn came up and joined them as I watched. All three of them stood looking at the tower as if suddenly unwilling to take the final steps of their long voyage into the past. I was struck by a sense of awesome antiquity as I watched their hesitation; but then, as I limped down from the rise and out toward the tower, the others seemed to break from the spell that bound them and moved to the ruin, putting out their hands to touch it.

After touching the ruin, Beorn stepped back and watched the others. I had a curious sense of unease as I looked at him. He seemed to be an observer rather than a partaker; more of the tower itself than of the exploration party.

As I came up, the professor was climbing carefully over a tumble of stones which had once been a wall. I passed Beorn and was nearly to Dot when I heard the professor's cry from beyond the tower wall. His voice curled over the broken stones of the tower like the screech of a great cat or the howl of a wounded dog. My hair stood on end and I spun toward the sound; even Beorn looked a bit startled.

"What is it?" Dot and I shouted together, as she scrambled over the stones toward the screams. The professor's head suddenly thrust over the wall in front of us, white with fury.

"It's been robbed!" he cried in rage and shock. "It's been dug out and robbed! Someone was here first, and they've dug out the whole thing! There's nothing left!"

Dot reached him then, and the two of them disappeared in a duet of unscholarly wailings on the far side of the wall.

I spun around and looked at Beorn, sliding my hand under my sweater. He was standing there with that look of ancient strength that I'd seen so often before. There was no longer any look of surprise on his face; only the professor's cry had startled him; he was not startled by the discovery that had caused the cry.

"It was you, wasn't it?" I said to Beorn, turning and easing myself down on a fallen stone so that I could face him and rest my bad knee.

He nodded his great head.

"Ya."

"It all fits," I said, thinking as I spoke. "That coin that Dot found down on the island; it's the same as the gold coin you had at the poker game, isn't it?"

"Ya, is the same," he rumbled. "But mine came from here, not from the island."

"How long have the Wiglafs known about this place?" I asked, feeling suddenly washed out and tired, and conscious of a simultaneous throbbing in my ears and knee.

He raised his brow, "Ah, Luther, my people have always known of this place." He gestured down toward the earth with his sausagelike forefinger, "This is Gotarland, the place of the old people—of my people."

The Luger was cold beneath my fingers, and I drew my

hand out from beneath my sweater without it. There seemed no use for the pistol now. Whatever damage Beorn might do had already been done; the anguished sounds of conversation and curses from behind the tower wall attested to that.

"What did you do with the treasure?" I asked. "That trail along the ridge is old. People have been coming here for a long time."

Beorn nodded, "For a thousand years, maybe, my father and his fathers have come here when trading is hard. They take a few gold coin when they sail. I do this too, when I sail on this last trip." He paused and then bared his great yellow teeth in a grin, "The gold here is gone now, I think; and you know who the man is who has the last of that gold? A little lawyer in Boston!"

I gestured toward the tower, "Will you tell them what you just told me?"

"Ya," he said, his grin still on his face. "You know, Luther, I thought it would be you who would find out what Beorn has done. It is not wise to let a man know too much of you, yes?"

"Maybe," I said, feeling very tired. Then I turned and called Dot and the professor. That must have been when Beorn hit me.

CHAPTER 14

I woke up slowly with the professor shaking me and shouting unintelligibly in my ear. Everything was fuzzy and out of focus; noise was diffused along with light with no sharp edges to sound or vision. Gradually though the professor's face came into focus and his noises began to form words.

"He's gone! Wake up, we've got to stop him! He's got Dottie, damn him! Wake up!"

I sat up and looked at him. A loop of Beorn's climbing rope still circled his upper arms where the big Scandinavian had tied him.

"Wake up, damn you!" shouted the professor.

"I'm awake," I said irritably. "What happened?"

"He's stolen Dottie! We've got to stop him! He has Dottie, I tell you!"

So that was what Beorn had in mind! "Where?" I asked.

"Back there." He waved a hand back inland along the ridge of the headland. "He trussed me up like a bag of potatoes, and I just got myself untied. He's been gone half an hour already! We've got to hurry!"

"Fat chance," I said, feeling my knee pushing against the elastic bandages which supposedly were holding it together.

I was in a violent mood and wasn't thinking clearly, "You're too old and I'm too stove up to catch a new-born baby."

The professor tore at the loop of rope surrounding him. "Dear God!" he raged, finally ripping the rope off and throwing it to one side. He staggered to his feet and tripped on another loop of rope. With a curse, he gathered up the rope in a haphazard armful of coils and knots, rushed to the cliff, and threw it off into space. With another curse he kicked a stone into space after it. "Damnation!" he cried. "Good riddance!"

"Very bright," I observed, my brain functioning at last. "You've just tossed away our chance to catch them, you chump!"

"Chump! Chump?" His eyes blazed, "What do you mean? What do you mean?"

"Well for God's sake," I snorted, "where do you think Beorn is taking her, anyway? He's going to his boat, of course! And to get there he's going to have to come right under this cliff, just like we did when we came up here. If we had that rope you just threw away, we could have scaled down the cliff and met him. If he's only been gone half an hour, like you say, he can't have gotten past the base of the cliff by now!"

"Good Lord," croaked the professor, clapping a hand to his forehead, "what have I done!"

"Just what you think," I said, reaching under my sweater. "However, you have nothing to fear; Old Luther is here." I pulled out the Luger, crawled to the lip of the cliff, and jacked a shell into the firing chamber, "I can pot anything that moves down there."

Nothing moved, and finally I said, "Tell me what happened, professor."

The professor was lying beside me, trying to see what was going to happen below the cliff. It was about a hundred and fifty feet straight down, and both of us were a bit skittish about the drop. Now and then we'd knock off little runs of sand or stone which would fall down out of sight scaring us silly.

"It's hard to say how it happened," he hedged. "When you called us, we were both terribly upset. . . ."

"I know," I said, "I heard."

He snorted, "Anyway, we came out from inside the tower and found you lying there and Beorn leaning over you. He said you'd fainted from the strain of climbing the headland, but that you were all right. Then he told us a long and very odd tale. He said . . ."

"Tell me later," I interrupted. "I can guess a lot of it. He probably told you that he'd been here before, right? And that he'd cleaned the place out, right?"

"Correct," said the professor in surprise. "How did you know?"

"We'll talk about that later," I said. "What happened after he told you his little tale of piracy?"

The professor seemed embarrassed, as would most men who'd been bundled up like a goat. "I hesitate to say, Luther, but I must admit that he caught me completely by surprise. . . ."

I touched the back of my head, "That's two of us, professor, so don't be bashful."

"Well, when he finished his story, Dot and I were, naturally, thunderstruck. Then he asked Dot if she would withdraw so he could speak to me in confidence. She did, and no sooner had she left than he grabbed me, stuffed a wad of cloth in my mouth, and wrapped me up in that damned rope. I tell you, Luther, the man is a monster of strength! I was completely helpless in his grasp!"

"I know what you mean," I said, watching below where Beorn had to be coming, but seeing nothing. Dot must be giving him problems, I thought, and felt my face redden: Him with my woman!

The professor went on, "While Dot was gone, he told me that he'd leave food and water for us here, and would leave the camp on the island for us to use until someone came for us. Blast the man! He even said he'd send someone to pick us up! Imagine the nerve! Then, when Dottie came back, he simply gave her a cuff, picked her up, and carried her off!"

"Just like an old Geat warrior, eh? Stole her away, eh?"

There was a pause, and then he said musingly, "By George, I believe you're right. That's probably just how it was done."

"With one small difference," I pointed out. "Beorn left us alive instead of dead."

"Well," said the professor, "he's not entirely uncivilized after all. . . ."

"He may live to regret his generosity," I said, hearing the clatter of a falling stone beyond the bend of the cliff to my right.

The professor had a sudden thought, "I'll get a couple of rocks and toss them down his way," he said. "That might frighten him into showing himself or letting Dottie go."

"No good," I said. "He'll have Dot right with him and he knows you'd never risk hurting her. What he doesn't know is that I have this Luger of his. I can probably get him if he and Dot aren't too close together when they come into sight."

"I hope you can shoot straight," whispered the professor as other sounds of movement came to us from beyond the bend in the cliff, "I don't want Dottie hurt!"

"Don't worry," I said, worrying. I'd never fired a Luger before.

Beorn came into view quite suddenly. He had Dottie by the wrist and was pulling her along behind him. Her clothes were rumpled and her hair was messed, so it was apparent that she had not come peaceably; but now she was being jerked along without too much resisting, so she'd run out of steam. Her glasses were missing, so she was probably half blind to boot. After having run up against her normal cool detachment off and on for five years, I must admit that the sight of her in disrepair somehow pleased me. But on the other hand she was, after all, my fiancée, my woman, and she was being stolen away from me by a man from another age. I laid the sights on Beorn's broad chest and tightened my finger on the trigger.

But then I decided that I didn't really want to kill him if I could help it, so I dropped the sights and aimed for his leg. Remembering that guns are supposed to shoot high when aimed downhill, I dropped the sights still farther, aiming for his foot with the intention of hitting him in the leg. I waited until he paused for a moment to negotiate a fallen boulder, aimed carefully, and squeezed off the shot. The pistol kicked up in my hand and the spent cartridge rattled against the rocks beside me as dust flew from between Beorn's feet and he, with a sweep of his tree-trunk arm, whipped Dottie off her feet, turned, and ran back toward the bend in the cliff which would hide him.

Dottie kicked and yelled, and Beorn tripped and fell. I aimed in front of him and shot into the dirt between him and the bend in the cliff, cutting him off from that escape. For an instant Dot broke away from him and I snapped the sights down on him for a quick shot. But I had no chance because he reached out again, caught her as she tried to roll away and whipped her back against his body. Dottie screamed with indignation and fright, and drove her elbow into his face. He laughed.

He had me spotted now, and kept Dot between us. Dot's flying arms and legs were bruising him, I was sure, in spite of his laughter, and he grimaced as a knee caught him in the groin. Then Dot reached for a rock, and Beorn, remembering what she had done to him during our fight in her room, probably regretted not having saved a bit of rope for her too.

Having no rope didn't bother him much, as it turned out. She was wearing a heavy woolen shirt, and Beorn reached out with a hamlike hand, caught her collar and jerked the shirt down, sending buttons flying and pinning her arms to her sides. Dot looked down at her bared bosom with shocked dismay. She had little time for shock on this account only, however, for in another instant he had jerked her belt from her dungarees, tied her wrists behind her back and slung her, bottom up, over his shoulder. Her hair fell out of its pins and tumbled in a dark swirl down his back.

High up on the cliff as I watched the two of them over the sights of the Luger, I had to admire his efficiency. In one minute Dot had been a furious whirlwind of angry fists, nails, and knees; in the next she was a squirming impotency whose most violent resistance was a breathless squeal of helplessness.

Beorn got to his feet and grinned up at me. The broadest target I had was Dottie's fanny where he had her draped over his shoulder. He waved his free arm and laughed. Dot writhed and started crying.

"The nerve of the bastard!" cried the professor furiously.

I waved back to Beorn. There really wasn't much else to do.

"Ah, my friend," roared Beorn, "you are awake, I see. You will forgive me if I take this woman." He slapped Dottie fondly on the rump, "She is a fine woman, I think. She will make a good wife, yes?"

Dottie wiggled like a worm and shouted something from beneath her flying hair.

"It's kidnaping!" I called. "That's a capital offense!"

He shrugged and laughed, "We will see, my friend. My first wife did not wish to go with me either, but we were soon happy together."

"She's my woman, you know," I yelled rather weakly. She wasn't really, and probably never had been.

"You are wrong, my friend. She is Beorn's woman now. I have taken her and I will keep her." He glanced at the sun, "I must go now. The tide is right for me when I get down to the boat."

"Blast you, Beorn!" shouted the professor. "Let that girl go!"

"Goodby, professor," boomed Beorn, walking sideways down the hill so as to keep Dottie's wriggling bottom between us. "If you start walking soon, you will be able to catch the low tide across the bridge to the island."

I tipped the muzzle of the Luger into the air and watched as he scrambled down the slope. His great shaggy head and bearlike body were massive and irrevocable as part of the earth as he stepped at last in under the trees and out of sight. Slung over his shoulder, bare-backed, and with loose hair streaming toward the ground, Dot seemed fragile and pale. At the last instant she tipped her head up and seemed to look back at us; but she could have seen nothing without her glasses, and it seemed to me that her last look was perhaps more of wonder than of fear.

The professor and I lay there for a while looking down into the forest where they had disappeared. Finally we crawled back from the edge of the cliff. I took the magazine out of the Luger, jacked the shell out of the chamber and put it in the magazine, and slapped the magazine back in the handle. The professor watched as I put the pistol back under my sweater.

"A fat lot of good that thing did you," he observed.

"Right you are," I said. "Still, we might have had him if things had been just a little different."

He looked at me with his cold blue eyes, "You know what I think? I think you didn't really intend to shoot him at all."

We sat there while I rubbed my knee. Finally he said, "Well, come on. Let's go up on the tower. We can see the fiord and the boat from there. We can watch them leave."

"Why not?" I said. Fat knee and all, I finally got up beside him on a wall facing the sea and looked down at the island. The boat seemed small.

I looked behind me at the inside of the broken tower. There was a hole in the center of the circle of walls, fallen rubble, and a great deal of blackened ashy soil.

"Beorn and his people have been coming here for generations," said the professor, following my gaze. "They took the coin away little by little whenever they needed trading goods. There's always a market for Roman gold.

"The dragon's hoard mentioned in the poem was probably the last of the coin and goods of the Roman colony on the island. The last survivor of that colony apparently removed it to the headland above the island and hid it away in the barrow there. There was probably little coin, actually; most of it must have been utensils, weapons, ornaments, and the like."

"Treasure?" I interrupted.

"That would have been treasure to anyone living on this coast at that time. The people of the Dark Ages knew the value of coin, of course, but other things were equally valuable and rare to them: good armor, weapons. Imagine what a find it would be for a Geatish warrior if he discovered a good Roman sword or Roman armor. Or a set of dishes, or a cup, or a chain of beads. Such things must have been beyond price to a people such as the Geats. They were in a hard, cold land where survival itself was almost impossible. They had neither the time nor the culture to produce things such as the Romans had."

"And now it's gone," I said, looking at the excavated floor.

"No," said the professor, with an unexpected note of satisfaction in his voice. "It really isn't. The gold is gone, of course, but everything else is still here. That black dirt there is really the most important thing we could have found, as far as I'm concerned."

I looked at him.

"It proves that there was a tremendous fire here when the tower was built. This charred earth is the final evidence that Beowulf really did live and die here. This is the spot where they burned his body and then erected the burial tower. With the evidence I have now, I can get financing for a proper archeological expedition to dig out the island, the barrow, and this tower!"

"Look down there," I said, pointing toward the fiord.

Below, like ants, we saw Beorn and Dottie come onto the beach. Beorn got the dinghy in the water, loaded Dottie into it, and rowed across to the island. There he beached the dinghy, went to camp for his and Dot's things, and then rowed to the *Gate of Horn*.

"You know where he got the name for his boat?" I asked. "He told me one time that his uncle used to sing an old song about two gates: one of horn and one of ivory. The gate of horn is where dreams pass that will come true, and the gate of ivory is where bad dreams pass."

"Homer," said the professor. "The *Odyssey*. Let me recall how it goes: Odysseus is speaking to Penelope of dreams, and she answers him that dreams are hard to understand. . . . Let me see, now . . .

> 'Twain are the gates of shadowy dreams,
> The one is made of horn, the other ivory;
> Such dreams as pass the portals of ivory
> Are deceitful, and bear tidings that are unfulfilled.
> But the dreams that pass through the gate of horn
> Bring true issue to whoever of mortals beholds them.' "

A stutter of sound came from the *Gate of Horn* as Beorn got her engine started. Dot was seated in the cockpit, and the sun gleamed white on her shoulders, proving that Beorn had not yet untied her. He was wise; Dot did not give in easily to anything.

The boat moved forward and Beorn pulled the anchor and stowed it. The tide was near its peak and there was little current. Going astern, Beorn cuffed Dot cordially on the cheek and took the tiller. The *Gate of Horn,* small as a toy in a bathtub, began to move through the gut between us and the island. Moments later she was heading out into the Kattegat and down the coast. In the distance the sound of her engine was lost in the wind and she looked like some ancient ring-prowed ship moving before hidden winds.

"Sutton Hoo," muttered the professor.

"Sutton who?" I asked, making a bad joke.

"Never mind," he said. "We'd better get started. Beorn says this fiord is three miles deep. That means we have six miles of walking before we get around to the bridge to the island. With your blasted knee, we'll be lucky to get there by low tide."

We climbed down, found the camera, stacked the tools against the tower wall, and started inland along the ridge of the headland. My knee hurt like hell, but I limped along as best I could. The professor stayed with me, muttering whenever I had to rest. It was a long walk, but we endured it with the odd comradeship of those who have suffered a common disaster.

CHAPTER 15

We'd been on the island for more than a week, and my knee was almost as good as new. Unable to leave, we'd taken pictures and done a bit more digging for artifacts to replace those Beorn had taken with the *Gate of Horn*. These, along with the notes and other film, we stored away in a small crate for safekeeping. Both of us were anxious to get back to the States before school started, but I was impressed by the fact that there was less personal irritability between us than I might have anticipated.

I was sitting on the seaward cliff fishing when I finally saw the sail. The boat stood in, growing larger and larger as it approached the island. It was a small, open sailboat with an outboard motor tipped up astern. Just outside the island, the lone sailor, a girl with golden hair, brought the boat into the wind, dropped sail neatly, and got the motor started. I ran down toward the camp, shouting for the professor.

By the time we got to the beach, the boat had come putting through the gut and was nosing in onto the sand. I caught a thrown anchor line and buried the anchor up on the beach.

"Welcome," I said.

"Thank you," she said, stepping ashore with a familiar-looking smile on her face. "My father contacted me after his honeymoon and asked me to come down and pick you two up."

"Your father?" asked the professor.

"Honeymoon!" I said.

"I am Wealhtheow Wiglafson," she said, smiling a golden smile at the professor. "He and Dorothy sent me to find you and bring you off the island."

She was big and lovely. I gaped at her without shame.

"Come along," she said. "We must get your things loaded aboard if we are to reach shore by nightfall."

I turned and went off to camp. Behind me I heard the professor ask bewilderedly, "How is Dottie? Is she well? She's not been hurt?"

The girl's great hearty laugh, a woman's lovely echo of Beorn's booming laughter, rolled across the fiord, "She looked well and happy when I last saw her, sir."

"Did she give you any message for me?"

"Only that she wished you and the young man there a safe trip home, and that you should not worry about her."

"I just can't believe it," said the professor.

"She is my father's woman," said the girl firmly. "You may believe that!"

I believed it.

We had the camp broken down and stowed in the boat in less than an hour. The professor looked around for stray items, then suddenly paused and touched my arm.

"Your sextant. It's on the *Gate of Horn*, isn't it? We can't leave here until I know precisely where we are! I've got to be able to get back."

I looked at him for a long moment, remembering all that had passed between us in the time we'd known each other. Then, with an oddly pleasant sense of resolution, I dug through my wallet and took out one of several folded pieces

We came in after dark to a little village the name of which
I never learned—possibly by design rather than chance. The
girl helped us load our gear into a panel truck before we
had a chance to speak to anyone, and soon had us all pounding inland over bumpy back roads. I bounced comfortably
beside her, rubbing against her as she drove, fascinated by
her size and grace. Beorn had said that his daughter was of
an age to be married, and he was absolutely right. I sensed
in her a timeless sensual vitality which drew me to her
much as Dottie had, I think, been drawn to her father.
Every now and then she would look quickly at me as I
swayed hip to hip beside her, and she would smile. On my
other side, the professor grunted and snorted in a semi-
sleep. He was not half so attractive.

By morning, when we caught a train at an obscure little
station which sat nestled in a grove of trees by a river, I
was reluctant to leave our hostess.

"Where do you live, Wealhtheow?" I asked.

She smiled, "I will be in Köbenhavn at the University for
two more winters."

"I'll come and see you," I shouted as the train pulled out
of the station toward Göteborg.

She lifted an arm in farewell and smiled her marvelous
smile as the train carried me away.

"Get your head inside, Martingale," grumbled the professor, who had not had a pleasant sleep during the ride in
the panel wagon.

"Wonderful big girl!" I said.

He snorted something, hunched down on his seat, and
closed his eyes. A few minutes later he began to snore. I
wasn't sleepy, however, and spent the day looking at Swedish scenery and wondering if Weststock had an exchange
program with the University at Copenhagen.

We were in Göteborg by five o'clock and on a plane south
toward Malmo and Copenhagen early the next morning.

In Copenhagen we bought tickets one way to the States. The professor had just enough money to get him home and I wasn't much better off. We were halfway across the North Sea when I brought up the subject of Weststock. I was certainly looking forward to attending the fall session, I said, and had every hope for a fine year.

He smiled oddly, "I've been considering our agreement about your readmittance to Weststock, Martingale. I was more or less blackmailed into helping you, you know. But now our relationship seems to me to have changed somewhat. You have served your purpose to me, after all, and I am, of course, grateful to you for that; but on the other hand you have been the cause of the loss of my niece and the expenditure of every monetary resource I have; you have lied about your health habits, about your morality, about your ownership of the boat, and, I suspect, about your devotion to academic studies. The objective reasons for continuing my efforts to get you into Weststock this term are therefore possibly of less merit than I may have believed this past spring."

He flashed his damned blue eyes at me, and smiled thinly, "For a number of years, as you know, I have disliked you intensely and could not imagine enjoying your presence on the Weststock campus. Had your plan of marriage to my niece been actualized I planned to make the best of it for her sake, but now that she has been carried off by that great Geat, Beorn, that possibility has evaporated. I am, therefore, free of susceptibility to either real or psychological coercion. It is a comforting experience, and one which leaves the mind free to function clearly."

He paused and suddenly became almost awkward, "What I am attempting to say, Martingale, is that I no longer feel threatened by you or driven by those private aspirations of mine which you so neatly played upon last spring. But more importantly for me, and I hope for you, is the unexpected fact that I find our recent weeks together have led me to believe that I will, in fact, not be at all displeased to share the Weststock campus with you this fall and in the years to come."

He ceased speaking suddenly as if out of breath but relieved to have gotten it all out. Open admissions of humanity exhaust certain kinds of otherwise decent college professors. I was touched.

"Thank you," I said, leaning back. Then, after a moment, "I hope you'll be equally willing to have me in your classes again."

He smiled his familiar dry smile, "Having attended them once already, you should do well, I imagine. I shall expect you to."

"Yes, sir," I said.

I felt comfortable. I was pleased that he had stuck to his bargain in spite of all. More than that, I was pleased that I'd made the right choice back on the island when he'd asked for the position of the place and I'd given it to him. Lying on the beach of the island where I'd dropped it, there might still be the other scrap of paper I'd made out at the time I'd written down the true position of the island. On that discarded paper were the longitude and latitude of Copenhagen; being no navigator, the professor would never have known the difference and I'd have had a lock on him in case he'd decided later to welch on his commitment to get me into Weststock.

But I'd given him the true readings and not the phonies and it had worked out anyway. I wondered now if I was getting soft or wiser, but was content with whichever it might be.

Below us the clouds, which floated like a blanket of cotton between us and the sea, opened for a moment and revealed the blue-black waters below. Looking down, I saw what seemed to be a sailboat beating westward into the wind. I blinked my eyes and tried to see it more clearly, but in that instant the cloud cover whipped back under the plane and the sea and ship were gone. I sat back and thought of Aunt Delia's inheritance, but somehow it seemed unimportant. My mind was caught between the bright vision of home and the dark antiquity of the Kattegat.

"In two years, we'll be ready to come back," said the professor suddenly, turning toward me.

"We?" I asked, startled.

"Well, of course," he said, a bit taken back at my tone. "You'll be graduated by then, and I'll have had time to organize the data we've collected, write a few papers, and arrange a first-class expedition. With the artifacts and photographs we have, we'll have no problem with funds this time." His eyes flashed with anticipation, "We'll knock the world's eyes out, my boy!"

I looked at him with pleasure. "Yes, sir," I said.